American Diaries

JOSIE POE

PALOUSE, WASHINGTON, 1943

———∞∞∞———

by Kathleen Duey

———∞∞∞———

Aladdin Paperbacks

For Richard
For Ever

J D8539jo

First Aladdin Paperbacks edition August 1999

Copyright © 1999 by Kathleen Duey

Aladdin Paperbacks
An imprint of Simon & Schuster
Children's Publishing Division
1230 Avenue of the Americas
New York, NY 10020

The text for this book was set in Fairfield.
Printed and bound in the United States of America
10 9 8 7 6 5 4 3 2

Library of Congress Catalog Card Number: 99-64163

ISBN 0-689-82930-2

Late Wednesday, July 14, 1943 . . . or no, I guess it is really the fifteenth now. It's about 2:30 A.M. I am sitting up and I've turned my lamp back on. Since I can't sleep, I may as well write.

An airplane went over low and it woke me up. For the longest time I could only lie here and pray that it wasn't a bomber. That newsreel at the Congress last week scared me—watching those poor English children running while the buildings just fell apart. I know the plane I heard was just from Felts or Leiger or some other airfield around here, but I can't stop imagining what will happen if the Japanese army invades us. I felt so sorry for the people of London back before we got into the war. How did they stand all those months when the German Luftwaffe was bombing them every single night? And now, there are people being bombed everywhere, it seems like. Everywhere but here.

I am going to try to stop thinking about the war for one night.

I still can't find my house key, and it has been almost a week. I would swear I put it on my dresser like I always do. I have to tell Daddy soon and I know he is going to be upset with me. Maybe I will wait until Mama is home on Tuesday. She told us when she called that she won't be driving back with Mr. Brand. He is leaving Sunday after the OPA meetings. So she will wait and take the train.

Mama called right after supper. She says Aunt Lila is doing better, and I am so relieved. It's been a strange week. Daddy has gone twice a day to make sure Mr. Brand's dairy herd is all right, checking on his hired help and making sure his wife doesn't need anything. They are having a terrible time, Daddy says. Unless this meeting in Spokane has changed something, the OPA won't let them charge more than a dime a quart for their milk, and feed prices are high this year. It'll be good when Mr. Brand is back and Daddy can stop running over there all the time. Daddy turned in early again tonight—I could hear him snoring when I was downstairs.

Tom is just getting worse. Heaven only knows where he was all day today. Daddy said at dinner that he was in the machine shed, working on the combine. But when I went to look, he was down in the cow barn, just sitting on a bale of hay, moping around like he has been so much lately—not working at all. He worries Mama. Daddy pretends not to notice much—but I think he is angry at Tom. I am.

Tom should just enlist. All his friends have. I am so sick of people asking me when he is going to go into the army—I never know what to say. That he *is waiting until the draft forces him in? If I were a man, I wouldn't wait to get drafted. I would just go fight.*

I forgot. I wasn't going to think about the war anymore tonight.

I wish I could have gone to Spokane with Mama. If she and Aunt Lila didn't need me, I would have spent one day at Natatorium Park. I LOVE that roller coaster and the bumper cars. I have only been once, but Tom has taken Evelyn Hanson there several times. Most of the high school kids go whenever they can, if someone has gas coupons to use. They get the BEST bands there!!

I am not that good a dancer yet, and I want to be. Girls who can dance like crazy always have dates! Tom used to practice with me, but not lately. Daddy hates dancing. He says he will dance once more in his life—at my wedding, and not before.

I will be glad to have Mama home for a selfish reason. I am tired of doing all the house chores by myself!! It has left me almost no time to do anything for fun. I know it is terrible of me to think about swimming at the plunge or going to an amusement park while the boys in the service are fighting and dying, though, and I shouldn't complain. There is a new poster at the library. It shows a dead soldier, fallen against a barbed-wire fence. The caption says,

"He knew the meaning of sacrifice." When you think about it that way, no one should ever complain about anything. The soldiers are the only ones who are really paying the price.

Last week I went with Frances and her mother to the Grange, and we rolled bandages. It was awful, sitting there thinking about the war, and the reason all the bags of bandages are needed. Mrs. Harris was there. She has two sons overseas now and she looks gray-faced and worried most of the time. She kept wiping her eyes, and Mama had to sit there looking straight ahead and pretending not to notice. And me, too. I just hummed to myself and rolled fast. I had a bigger pile of bandages finished than anyone else when we ran out of cotton strips. If we had one GI in the family, then I would feel the same as Frances and Ginnie and Mary—and practically all my other friends whose brothers and cousins have gone in. There were twenty-eight in the graduating class this year at the high school, and only four of them were boys—counting Tom. All the rest had already gone to war. Nearly every family in town has sent someone, except us.

I just reread all that and I know I would be mortified if Tom ever saw it. But it's true. I just feel so ashamed that he still isn't even trying to enlist. No wonder Evelyn broke off with him. All the girls are crazy about uniforms now. Larry Mellon enlisted before graduation. Phil Bass did, too, two weeks ago. He went down for his induction physical last week, Tom said. Larry and Phil and Tom have done everything together since they went to first grade in the old school on the footpath. Mama used to call them the three-headed monster—they were together that much.

I am determined to think of something spectacular to do for the war effort. Last Wednesday, down at the Oasis, Frances and I were trying to come up with ideas. We read in the Palouse Republican about kids in New York City doing grand things—collecting tons and tons of paper and old tires. But here??? The boys are all out selling war bonds at their rallies for the band and next year's teams. The high school girls and the Gang a' Gals club are on a letter-writing campaign. I spend a lot of time in our Victory Garden watering and hoeing, and I just planted the second crop of lettuce and green onions. We haven't had to buy vegetables at all this summer. Mama and Daddy say that everyone's contributions help and that we'll win the war because we are all so determined to beat Hitler and the rest of the Axis. But I just feel like I need to do something bigger than weed a stupid garden. Anything!

I can hear another plane, I think. It's very faint, very far away. My heart is pounding, anyway. The bombing could come here, too, any day, just like at

Pearl Harbor. There are rumors of bombs coming in on helium balloons, even though we aren't supposed to gossip about stuff like that. The sound of the plane is gone now. I hate feeling scared like this.

I really, REALLY want to think of something good to do. In the "Gifts for the Brits" drive at the end of the school year, people collected coats and soap and toiletries, so Frances and I figure it is too soon to do something like that again.

I wonder if the war will go on until I am grown?

Ooops. I hear the front door creaking open. So I guess Tom is finally home. I had better put this away so he won't see it if he looks in on me. He probably won't. He has barely said ten words to me in the last week. God, if you are listening, I understand that my brother is probably scared to go. I would be, too, but I would do it, and he needs to, too. Please help him be brave enough to enlist and let us win this lousy war soon.

CHAPTER ONE

Josie got up, threw back her blanket, and ran to hide her diary at the bottom of her sweater drawer. Then she spun around, tiptoeing back to lie on her bed. She closed her eyes and concentrated on slowing her breathing, relaxing her hands and her expression. It would take Tom a minute to get upstairs. She would have time to do a good job of pretending to be asleep if he looked in on her.

As Josie listened for Tom's footsteps, there was an odd clunking sound out in the yard, then twenty or thirty seconds of silence. Had he gone back outside? She only had a moment to wonder before she heard Tom's footfalls downstairs again. They got louder, then softer again as he turned into the kitchen. He paused at the icebox—she heard the door open and close, too quickly for him to have taken anything out. He had either changed his mind or seen the pies on the sideboard.

A tiny rattle—the sound of the silverware drawer

being pulled out—told her she was right about the pies. Tom was always hungry. And since no one was up to scold him for it, he would just cut a big piece and take it upstairs with him.

There was silence from the kitchen a moment later, then Josie heard her brother's footsteps as he came back out into the hall. He walked slowly, coming past the telephone table, then into the sitting room at the base of the stairs. After another second or two, she heard him start upward.

For a few seconds, Josie regretted not turning off her lamp, knowing Tom would see the narrow band of light that leaked from beneath her door. But he would have seen that her window was lit from outside, anyway, so he would know she had snapped the light off when she heard him coming. She lay still. If he knocked, she would pretend it had awakened her. That way he wouldn't tell Daddy she was up so late.

Daddy got so worried about everything lately. He wouldn't get angry, he would just lecture her, then tell Mama, then Mama would worry. . . . Then they would both be watching to see that she went to sleep at a decent hour—and she just couldn't lately. She often read for hours before she felt drowsy.

On the heels of that thought, Josie sat up just enough to reach for her bookshelf. She pulled down the novel she had been reading and laid it facedown next to her as Tom topped the stairs. The floor creaked a little as he came across the landing. Josie tried to even out her breathing as he stopped outside her door.

"Josie?" It was barely a whisper. She pressed her lips together.

"Josie?"

Tom's whisper was a little louder now, and she heard her door click as though he was leaning against it from the other side. "Josie?"

She held her breath.

"Josie Posie?" he said in a singsong voice. "Are you asleep?"

She remained still, feeling her cheeks flush. She hated that old nickname, and he knew it. He was using it as a test to see if she was really asleep. After a long, quiet pause, she heard him walk away. Then, the familiar two-tone squeak of his door hinges told her that he was going into his own room, closing his door behind him.

Josie frowned. He hadn't even peeked in at her. She was glad, but she was upset with him, too. He used to keep an eye on her.

"And you used to get mad at him for it," she whispered to herself as she stood up.

She went to the window. The moon was full tonight, bright enough to cast shadows. She cupped her hands around her face and looked out. The yard looked ghostly and strange. The old, horse-drawn plow and the hay wagon were outlined in a silvery light that made the shadows beneath them ink-black and mysterious.

Off to the other side of the yard was the rusted truck and the Buick that Daddy insisted on keeping instead of adding to the war effort. There was a toothed harrow that was so old, the steel was nearly rusted through in places. Daddy said the plow and the harrow were too far gone for the scrap drives, but she knew there was more to it than that. They had belonged to Daddy's grandfather when he had first farmed here in Whitman County.

Josie shivered, even though it wasn't cold. She wished she could go downstairs and call Frances and try to explain how strange she felt tonight. But, of course, she couldn't call now, in the middle of the night.

"Or in the middle of the day," Josie whispered, frowning. "Not for something personal like this."

Even though Frances wasn't on a party line, Josie was—and there was always Mrs. Hagan to worry about. She often picked up her phone when someone else was on the line so she could eavesdrop. Then she would gossip about whatever she heard. Mama had no use for her, even though she was always polite if they met in public. Daddy said Mrs. Hagan was lonely and didn't have enough family of her own to keep her occupied.

Another sudden two-note creak made Josie freeze, scattering her thoughts. In four quick steps she was lying on her bed again, feigning sleep. As she lay still, her eyes closed, she listened intently, sorry she hadn't turned off her light when she'd had the chance.

This time Tom's footsteps were slower, heavier, and Josie thought for a few seconds that he had stopped in front of her door. She tried to force a sleepy, relaxed expression onto her face. Then, she heard Tom move toward the head of the stairs again. This time, she could not keep track of his footfalls as he went downward. It dawned on her that he was trying to be quiet! Why? He knew that Daddy never woke up unless someone roused him.

Josie felt her stomach tighten. Tom was trying not to waken *her*. That made even less sense. He was never outright rude about clomping up and down the stairs, but he never tiptoed, either.

The instant Tom's footsteps faded as he went down the stairs, Josie jumped up. When she heard the front door open, she ran to her window. Staying to one side, not sure why she was being so wary, she leaned forward by inches, like Dick Tracy in the movies, just far enough to peek down into the yard. At first she could only see shadows and darkness, but then her eyes adjusted. What she saw made her catch her breath.

Tom was walking across the yard, headed toward the open cow field east of the house. He was carrying something. She squinted, trying to see what it was, but she couldn't. He was walking slowly, leaning back a little. At the edge of the yard, he ducked through the barbed wire, then turned back and faced the house for an instant. Then he started off again, walking fast until he disappeared into the dark.

Josie could only stare, peering out her window, wishing the moon were brighter. What in the world was Tom up to in the middle of the night like this? He was only getting away with it because Mama was gone. Daddy would sleep through a house fire and a herd of buffalo on the stairs, but Mama woke up if the wind sighed—and Tom knew that every bit as well as she did.

Josie flopped down on her bed, then glanced at the little windup clock that ticked quietly on her desk. It was almost three o'clock. Mama would be angry if she knew that neither one of her children was asleep at this hour.

Josie took out her diary again and held it against her chest. She was so grateful to Aunt Lila for having given it to her on her last birthday. Keeping a journal was a pretty frivolous use of paper, she knew. But it was an old diary that Aunt Lila had never used. It had been made long before the war, so it wasn't like she was taking paper production away from the armed services.

Sometimes, writing in the diary helped her sleep. It was hard not to think about the war, and bombs, and all the men who were dying every minute of every day—and it was worse at bedtime. Writing about other things helped her keep her mind off the war long enough for her to go to sleep.

But what could she write now? That her brother was up to something very strange? That she was only awake this late because a plane had gone over and scared her? Josie slid the diary beneath her pillow and walked to her dresser to snap off her light.

The darkness was close and uncomfortable, and she sighed. Whatever Tom was up to, he would not appreciate her interference. He was five years older than she was—he was eighteen and a man now—old enough to be drafted.

Sighing, Josie looked out her window once more, this time standing squarely in front of it, knowing that without the light behind her she was invisible to anyone outside—her window would be a black rectangle. It was like a blackout, she thought, then chided herself. Thinking about how people on the coast were pulling heavy cloth across their windows at night so bombers couldn't use city lights as a target was not exactly going to make her sleepy.

Staring down into the moonlit yard, Josie said a prayer, pleading with God to end the war soon. She knew that hundreds of thousands of other people whose countries had Allied forces fighting all over the world were probably praying the exact same thing at that exact instant. Mama always said she was sure there were plenty of German and Italian and Japanese people who didn't want the war to continue, either. Josie just wished that somehow all the prayers would add up so the war would soon be won and over with.

Tom's sudden appearance at the edge of the yard startled Josie into stepping back from the window. He walked toward the house, empty-handed now. A few seconds later she heard the kitchen door open and close, softer this time. Maybe Daddy wasn't snoring as loudly now, and Tom wasn't sure if he was sleeping deeply.

Josie wondered what Tom had carried out—then come back without. Maybe he was taking things out to his old secret place—the way he had when he was younger. She knew more or less where it was from when she used to spy on him. The place was Tom's big secret, up a little draw at the far end of the farm, where the rolling hills gave way to the rocky hillsides and scattered pines.

As Josie listened, Tom came up the stairs, and she lay down on her bed again but kept her eyes open.

He went past her door without pausing, then went into his own room. She heard him moving around for a minute or two, then the house was silent again, and she was left alone in the dark with her uneasy thoughts.

CHAPTER TWO

The morning sun was streaming in the window when Josie opened her eyes. She sat straight up. Her father rose every day at dawn and clomped up the stairs to wake her and Tom. She could not remember the last time she had slept in.

Josie swung her feet to the floor. Her clock read ten of seven! She shook her head in disbelief, then crossed her room to her armoire. It had been her grandmother's and she loved it, even though it wasn't modern like the built-in closets at Frances's house.

Taking out her favorite everyday dress, Josie listened, wondering if Tom and her father were up. They had to be by now, but the house was silent. That in itself was unsettling. Daddy never slept in, and from the second he was up he had the radio on, listening to the farm reports.

Josie pulled the bright yellow rayon dress over her head. Mama had let it out once and lengthened the hem twice. The fabric was still sound and sturdy, and the yellow was almost as bright as it had been the day she and Mama had bought it at Williamson's a year before.

Josie remembered how proud she had been of the dress the first day of school that year. Afterward, Tom had actually taken her with him into town to visit Louise Tallen, his girlfriend back then. Louise had suggested that they all walk downtown for an ice cream.

She had skipped ahead as they had waltzed down the footpath and across the footbridge. She had held her head high coming up Beach Street. She had felt so grown up and so happy to be with Tom and Louise that day. But more than anything she had felt so patriotic wearing rayon! Cotton and silk were needed for tent canvas and parachutes.

"Josie!"

Daddy's voice through the bedroom door was abrupt and impatient. Startled, Josie spun around, then crossed her room. "Yes? I'm almost dressed."

"Come down quick as you can," he said in the same agitated tone.

"Coming!" she shouted back, then turned back to her armoire. Something *was* wrong, she was sure of it now. But, what? Heart thudding, her hands flying over her shoelaces, she tried not to think about what it could be. Had there been a telephone call in the night? Their ring was three short and two long—so it was usually enough to wake her, even though the phone was downstairs. Had something happened to Aunt Lila or Mama? Or Tom? As soon as she thought it, Josie remembered the night before, watching Tom cross the yard. Had he gone back out? Maybe he had gotten hurt rambling around in the dark. Maybe Daddy had run him into the doctor's and that was why he hadn't awakened her at six as usual. Josie shook her head to scatter her worried thoughts and ran to the top of the stairs.

Going down in a quick, hammered rhythm, she turned the corner at the landing, then descended the last six steps two at a time.

"Whoa!"

Tom's voice startled her, and she looked up to meet his eyes. He smiled a little, but the expression did not spread beyond his lips. His eyes were narrowed and tense. He waggled his finger at her. "Where's the fire?"

"Daddy sounded so upset, I thought you were . . . I thought someone might be . . . " Josie trailed off. He was still wearing the thin half-smile, an expression she could never remember seeing on his face before. It made him look unfamiliar. "I thought someone was hurt or something," she finished.

He arched his eyebrows without saying anything. She heard the kitchen door open and close, then the sound of her father's heavy footsteps coming into the living room.

"Good, Josie, you're here," Daddy said, and Josie turned to see him coming up the hall. "Did you see or hear any trespassers out in the yard last night?"

"No," Josie said without thinking. Then she glanced at Tom as her father went on.

"Well, we've had a robbery, of sorts."

She looked back at her father. "A robbery?"

He nodded. "Someone broke into the old Buick. I had a five-gallon gas can in there for emergencies—full to the brim. And that old tent of your grandpa's that we use for fishing," he added, then paused and scratched his head. "I haven't had anything stolen off this place in fifteen years. The only other time I can recall was that hay fork one of the wheat crew walked off with."

"Maybe there were train tramps through here last night," Tom said quietly.

"You said that before," Daddy responded, eyeing Tom sharply. Josie shot him a look, too. Maybe that's what he had been doing—giving supper to road bums. He always asked Mama for food when they came to the back door. She usually said yes even though Daddy didn't like it. But the tramps had never stolen anything before.

"If neither of you saw anything—" Daddy began, but Tom interrupted him.

"I might have, now that you remind me of it."

"You saw someone? Why didn't you say so an

hour ago?" Daddy demanded, running one hand back through his hair. It was obvious that he hadn't combed it yet.

"I didn't *see* anyone," Tom answered. "I thought I *heard* something, then I decided I had imagined it. I woke up around two, maybe later. There was a—"

"There was a plane," Josie interrupted, her sleepiness beginning to fade. "It woke me up, too." She looked at her father. "I got scared thinking about bombs."

"You always do," Tom said flatly, and Josie looked back at him, trying to read his eyes. He was scared, too. If he wasn't, why hadn't he signed up with the army or the marines like all his friends had?

"What did you hear?" Daddy asked Tom.

Josie heard the curt tone in her father's voice. He would never listen to her worry out loud about bombings or the Japanese army attacking from the coast. Mama said it was because thinking about it scared him, too. It scared everyone.

"I don't know exactly," Tom said finally, speaking slowly. "It was a thumping sound, and I thought it was from out in the yard somewhere. But then I realized it was probably just Josie Posie the night owl here, banging around in her room."

"Don't call me that," Josie snapped at him.

"Don't call you what? Josie Posie?" Tom repeated evenly.

"You know I hate it."

"You do?" He was smiling innocently now.

"Cut it out, you two," Daddy said.

Josie glared at her brother. He was eighteen years old. Old enough to be a soldier. And he was acting like a ten-year-old. He knew very well how much the nickname bothered her. Josie clenched her hands into fists, then released them before Daddy could notice. He was already upset enough without her adding to it. Once more, Josie wished her mother was home. Whenever there was an emergency, Mama always managed to calm everyone down, to make things seem right again.

"Dad?" Tom said suddenly.

Daddy blinked. "What?"

"We need to get the combine blades sharpened. And maybe reset. I can't do that on my own."

Daddy looked thoughtful. "Okay. You told me that a couple of days ago. I'll call Davis to come out."

Josie listened to her father and brother talking about getting the work done on the combine as her thoughts whirled along a very different path.

She was pretty sure that Tom had been outside walking around in the middle of the night, taking supper plates to hoboes who had thanked him with a robbery. Josie closed her eyes for a second, then opened them. There weren't nearly as many tramps since the war started. That was why Daddy didn't want Mama to feed the ones they did see. He said that the tramps used to be honest men down on their luck—but now, with the war on, anyone who couldn't find work was either lazy, foolish, or flat unable to do any kind of job at all.

Josie looked at Tom. He had a stubble of thin whiskers on his chin, and his eyes were puffy from lack of sleep. If he had given the tramps supper, he had only been doing what Mama would have done. And, Josie admitted to herself, if he had asked for her help, she would have given it to him without hesitation. But it looked like Daddy was right. Maybe the tramps weren't honest men anymore.

Daddy noticed her looking toward them and shook his head. He looked furious.

"Should I make us some breakfast?" Josie asked, trying to do what Mama would have done to get things back on track.

Daddy shook his head. "I can't eat yet. I just walked out this morning to watch the sunrise like always," he began. "Then I noticed the trunk of the Buick standing open." He said it in a tight, growling voice, and Josie could tell how angry he was. "I've been chasing my tail ever since, wishing I could find whoever had the gall to come into my yard and steal like that. As soon as it got to be a decent hour, I called Pete Parnell."

"You called the sheriff?" Tom asked.

Josie glanced at her brother. His face hadn't changed. He was still standing casually with his hands in his pockets. But there was an odd intensity in his voice and eyes.

"Of course I did," Daddy answered. "We were robbed, son." He said the last few words in a sarcastic voice.

"But it was just an old tent and some gasoline," Tom said.

"Someone jimmied that trunk open. It could just as easily have been the back door!" Daddy exploded.

Josie could not stop staring at her brother. If he *had* fed some hoboes the night before, he wouldn't want to admit it now that they had turned out to be dishonest. But if Sheriff Parnell got involved, he might just have to.

"Not that it'll do much good," Daddy was saying. "Pete says he'll have Ora Rees or one of the other deputies drive down to check along the tracks by the upgrade. If they're down there trying to jump a train, the deputy'll see them. But if they already hopped a night freight, they're long gone."

"There were three or four trains last night," Tom said quickly.

Josie held her breath as she watched her father's frown deepen. She hadn't heard a single train, had she? Daddy's sunburned face was tense and troubled, and for an instant Josie hated the hoboes for upsetting him like this. There was enough wrong in their house and in the world without extra problems.

"I don't like losing that old tent," Daddy said, pushing his hair back again. "It was my father's. It didn't look like much, but you can't buy canvas now for love nor money. I guess they'll probably pitch it somewhere for a night or two, then leave it in the hills to rot when they don't want to carry it anymore. It probably weighs forty–fifty pounds."

"They're probably long gone on a freight by now," Tom said slowly, shrugging. "I heard one coming up the grade around two-thirty or so."

Josie stood very still, unsure of what to say or do. Tom was shaking his head, a sad expression on his face. But there hadn't been a freight train around two-thirty, had there? Josie tried to remember. She had been wide awake then, listening for the sound of bombing. She could not have missed a train whistle, could she?

"Well, I suppose there's nothing to do about it but wait for Pete to get here. Let's get on with the chores." Daddy pushed his hair back once more, angrily, as though it had better learn not to fall in his eyes, or else. Then he heaved a big sigh. "Josie, would you start breakfast now, please? I am mad enough to chew nails, so I may as well eat."

It was a silly joke, the kind Daddy often made, and Josie smiled at him. "Sure. Oatmeal or—"

"Eggs, this morning, Josie," Daddy said. "And fry a little of the bacon I got down at West's, will you? It's grocery store bacon, but it's better than the butcher's."

"It's leaner," Josie said automatically, echoing what Mama would have said if she had been there.

Daddy didn't answer, and Tom was already edging away, moving toward the front door. "I'll start watering and feeding," he said. "Cows first?"

Daddy nodded as Tom left. "I'll be down to help in a minute."

Josie started toward the kitchen, but her father stopped her. "What's all this about you being awake last night?"

"The plane," Josie began, then she stopped and looked straight into his eyes. "Sometimes I just start thinking about the war and I can't sleep."

Daddy looked at her for a long time, then he nodded. "It'll be worse when our Tom is over there. I hope your mother can bear up."

Josie tried to think of something to say, but Daddy was already looking past her. "I'll find my hat and get on down to help Tom. I've got time?"

"Breakfast in about twenty minutes," Josie told him. He nodded and went around her, purposeful and somber. Josie watched him go, thinking about what he had said. It *would* be worse when Tom was gone. But it would be better in a way, too. At least she wouldn't feel like everyone in town was sacrificing more than her family was. She sighed and headed for the kitchen.

Flipping on the light, she saw the little mess her father always left when he made the coffee. Mama said he made wonderful java, but he needed an assistant—someone to clean up after him.

Josie suddenly missed her mother sharply. She blinked back tears as she wiped up the scattered coffee grounds, then set about cooking. By the time the bacon was sizzling in the frying pan, she was feeling better.

She decided to call Frances right after breakfast and ask if they could get together and work on their plan to do something big for the war effort. Maybe, if they thought of something good enough, they would end up in the "This Week" section of the Sunday papers like those kids from New York City. Maybe the *Palouse Republican* would do a big article on them— or at least Guy La Foulette would mention them in his "About the State" column.

Josie allowed herself to daydream while she mixed and poured orange juice and sliced bread for the first batch of toast. She imagined herself and Frances being applauded at the Grange hall after a dinner held to recognize their efforts. Then the whole town would know that the Poe family was doing its part to win the war.

While Josie set the table, she imagined how it would be when the war was over and how wonderful it would feel to know that the killing and dying had stopped. It would be terrific to feel like she really had helped win the war.

The front door banged open, and Daddy came in, smiling at the warm smell of the bacon and eggs. "I could eat old socks," he said, making one of his favorite jokes.

Since Mama wasn't there to laugh at it as he went down the hall to wash up, Josie did. She got a plate out of the cupboard and set it on the counter. Glancing at her father, she put six strips of bacon on it, still sizzling with grease. Then she broke four big brown eggs into the bubbling bacon fat. The edges curled like petticoats, and she gently used the spatula to slosh the hot fat over the tops of the eggs—turning them white almost instantly.

Josie lifted the eggs from the skillet while they were still soft in the center—the way her father liked them. She slid them off the spatula onto his plate, carefully placing them next to the bacon strips.

A few seconds later, he came back up the hall from washing his hands, just as the phone rang. Josie peeked out the kitchen door. The first three rings, all long, made him pause. When the next two were short, he plucked the receiver from its cradle and held it over his ear. She couldn't hear what he was saying over the sound of the sizzling bacon. Biting her lower lip, she turned back to the stove.

"I have to go into town after breakfast," Daddy said half a minute later, coming into the kitchen. "Mrs. Brand needs disinfectant. One of their hands smashed a whole crate of it. Dropped it. That woman is going to come apart if her husband isn't back soon."

"Will you take me into town when you go, Daddy?"

He grunted as he sat down, and Josie slid his plate onto the table. "Where? To Frances's house?"

Josie nodded. "If her parents say it's all right. I haven't called yet." She turned to the toaster to pull out the warm bread. It was hard to handle the thin slices without them falling apart. That was one thing she would look forward to after the war. *Thick* slices of bread. She put the toast on a smaller plate for her father, pushing the jam jar close enough for him to reach.

"You and Frances going to go swim?"

"Maybe," Josie told him. "But I mostly want to think up some terrific thing to do for the war effort."

Josie watched her father nod approvingly. "It all adds up," he said, taking his first bite of egg.

Josie sliced more bread and dropped it into the toaster, but before she could touch the lever, Daddy spoke. "Hold up on Tom's," he said around a mouth full of eggs. He lifted his orange juice glass, then wiped his mouth with his napkin. "He said he had a couple of things to do before he came in."

Josie nodded, puzzled. Tom was usually the first one at the table and the last one to leave. He never skipped a meal, and he never got there late. But if Daddy thought it was strange, too, he didn't say anything.

CHAPTER THREE

All the way to town, Daddy was silent. Then, dropping her off in front of Frances's house, he finally spoke. "You'll be home in time to cook supper?"

Josie nodded. "Probably before. Frances and I might go swim for an hour, but then we're going straight to her house to talk about our war effort ideas."

Daddy nodded vaguely, turning the car up Church Street in a wide, smooth arc.

"I really want to do something important," Josie said into the silence as Papa turned left onto H Street and slowed, crawling the last block to Frances's house. When he braked to a gentle stop, Josie leaned over to hug him.

"I don't want you to go telling everyone you meet about the robbery," he said as she straightened up. "I know you'll tell Frances, but let it go at that."

Josie blinked. "Why?"

Her father shrugged. "It isn't the whole town's business, that's all."

Josie could see a stubble of beard on his chin. He hadn't shaved. He hadn't changed out of his work clothes, either. Mama wouldn't want him coming to town like this, Josie knew. Mama was very proper about appearances.

"I'll start home long before dark," Josie said, glancing at France's front door. She slid across the seat, reaching for the handle. It was loose, and she had to concentrate for a second to line it up right so that the latch would release. She glanced at Frances's lovely house as she got out, then back at the dented fender of the Ford sedan. Daddy loved this old car, she knew, but maybe after the war, when they were selling cars again, he would think about buying a newer one. "If you're going to be late, be sure to call," Daddy said as she got out.

"I will, Daddy," she promised.

"Make sure you don't run past four or so starting back out toward home," he went on. "The last thing we need is you getting into some kind of trouble."

"Okay, Daddy," she said, dancing from one foot to the other. He was making it sound like she was going to be a thousand miles away or something. It was a three-mile walk. It would take her less than an hour.

"You have your key?"

The question startled her, and she ducked her head, not really nodding. "Daddy, I have to go now.

I told Frances half an hour and I'm already late."

Before he could say anything else, she turned and ran, cutting across the lawns, then turning up the sidewalk that led to Frances's front door. She heard her father grind the Ford into gear, and she waved without breaking stride.

The brass knocker was cold to Josie's touch, even though the morning was sunny and warm. Fidgeting, she counted to twenty before the door finally opened.

"Hello, Josie," Frances's mother said in her soft, ladylike voice. She was dressed like she was going to church. She probably had a board meeting or something to go to this morning. She belonged to most of the clubs in town, Josie was sure. It seemed like she had a meeting every day of the week. She was in the Xenodican Club. They helped the library and raised money for all sorts of community doings. She belonged to the Gang a' Gals club, too. They always had some project going on.

"Hello, Mrs. Keener." Josie lifted her head up and tried to look and sound polite and ladylike, too.

"Good morning, Josie. Frances is in her room. You may run on up if you like." Mrs. Keener took a step back so Josie could come in.

"Thank you, ma'am," Josie said stiffly. She walked toward the staircase that rose grandly out of the entryway.

Glancing over her shoulder, Josie saw Mrs.

Keener going back into the kitchen. Frances had such a perfect family. Her father worked at Williamson's department store and he was always clean and looked like a gentleman. Her eldest brother, Jim, was fighting in France somewhere, and Jack, who was seventeen, was working in a munitions plant in Spokane for the summer.

Josie hurried up the stairs, aware, as always, of the deep, soft carpet beneath her feet. She loved being in Frances's house, but she was never quite comfortable. Mrs. Keener was just too perfect. Her hair was always smooth and shining, and her clothes were always beautifully fitted and pressed—always made of good fabric. Her nails were filed into smooth, round curves, never ragged from gardening or forking hay like Mama's often were. Mrs. Keener had never lived on a farm.

Going down the upstairs hall, Josie heard the telephone ringing below. Out of habit she slowed her step and tried to hear the ring pattern, then realized there was no need to do that here. The phone line into this house served only one family. The operator would just send single, longish rings until someone picked up—and if no one did, she would tell the calling party that no one seemed to be answering. The next ring was cut short, and Josie heard Frances's mother's calm voice saying good morning to the caller.

"Psst!"

Josie looked up and saw Frances grinning at her. She was wearing her bathrobe still, and Josie felt another tiny stab of jealousy. No one ever woke Frances at dawn to help with chores. Her father didn't even go into Williamson's to work until eight-thirty.

Josie followed Frances down the carpeted hall, their footsteps hushed. France's bathrobe almost brushed the floor. Mrs. Keener had made it, Josie knew. She was a wonderful seamstress and she could afford to buy the best fabrics to work with. The robe was a beautiful rayon velvet, the deepest, richest purple that Josie had ever seen. Frances opened her room door and crooked her finger at Josie, making a clownish gesture for her to follow.

As usual, Frances's room was as neat as a pin. Josie sighed and promised herself that one day soon she would clean her own room thoroughly and then would redecorate and maybe even repaint it if Daddy would buy paint for her. She had made herself the promise a hundred times. She wondered if she would ever keep it. Mama would help, if she could find the time. But there would be little money for fancy curtains and framed pictures for the walls, she knew. Her room would never look like Frances's.

"What time do you have to go home?" Frances asked.

Josie smiled. That was always the first question

Frances asked. "I have to start back at four or so."

"Walking?" Frances arched her brows.

Josie nodded.

"Did you tell anyone what we are planning on doing?"

"I told Daddy it was something for the war effort." Josie shrugged. "How could I tell him any more than that when we don't even know what we want to do yet?"

Frances nodded. "When we do have ideas, I want to keep them to ourselves for a while. Until we really decide on something."

Josie smiled again. Ever since they had become friends in Mrs. Hullet's third-grade class, Frances had loved making up secrets. But she was terrible at keeping them. She would be the one who spilled the beans first, Josie would have bet anything on it.

"But we can't just do the same old things," Frances was saying. Josie looked up, and Frances grinned at her. "You look daydreamy. What were you thinking about?"

"Third grade," Josie said, laughing. "That time we had to stay in from recess for passing notes."

Frances nodded. "Everything was fun back then. No one had to save every little piece of string, and we didn't use ration books, and no one was afraid and—"

"Before the war," Josie interrupted.

"Before the war," Frances echoed. Then she looked up at the ceiling, and Josie knew she was thinking about her brother.

Josie sat carefully on the edge of Frances's ruffled bedspread. "We should try to do something that will really make a difference," she said quietly.

Frances nodded enthusiastically. "But people have already done almost everything. . . . "

"We just have to organize everything perfectly," Josie said.

Frances twirled around on one foot, her arms up like a ballerina's. "But what?" She whirled around again. "It needs to be flamboyantly spectacular."

Josie nodded, smiling a little. Frances was great at throwing big words into everyday sentences. She wanted to be a writer. "Help me, Josie!" Frances scolded suddenly. "Think!"

Josie blushed. "I'm trying. It was my idea that we should do *something*."

"Having the idea to get an idea doesn't count!" Frances said, laughing, and Josie had to giggle with her. But it was Frances who stopped laughing first. "Maybe a bake sale and we can sell war stamps along with the cakes?"

"The Masons had a pastry booth at the last Grange Victory Day."

Frances's face fell. "Well, what, then?"

"I don't know," Josie admitted. "I was awake half

the night, thinking. I tried to come up with something and I couldn't."

"Maybe there isn't anything different left to do," Frances said, sighing. "People have collected everything—stockings, scrap metal, paper, copper, even golf balls." She frowned.

Josie looked at her closely. Sometimes Frances got discouraged if things were too hard. Josie didn't want that to happen this time. She needed Frances. It would be impossible to pull off anything as good by herself as she could manage with Frances helping.

"Maybe we should have a scrap metal drive," Josie said, just wanting to say something to keep Frances going. "The Boy Scouts did it a couple of years ago, remember?"

"But you said you wanted to do something new and different," Frances said.

Josie nodded. "But no one has held a metal drive since then," she answered. "I mean, besides everyone canning their own fruit to save using tin and steel to make cans."

"If anyone has, I haven't heard about it," Frances said.

"Me either," Josie agreed.

"My mother canned peaches last year," Frances said proudly.

Josie nodded and bit her lip. Her own mother had canned peaches, apples, applesauce, tomatoes, berries, rhubarb, and more the year before—and she would again come August. She had an application in for a new pressure canner and Josie was pretty sure she would get one. Then she would be able to put up corn and beans and squash.

Frances arched her perfect eyebrows. "But Mr. Quiggle at the Riverside garage is buying all the scrap that anyone brings in, isn't he?"

Josie shrugged. "Maybe, but people only think of the big things for selling like that. We want every little bit of metal scrap. We want people to go through their sheds and attics and junk drawers and—that's it!" She snapped her fingers and grinned.

"What's 'it'?" Frances demanded.

Josie leaned forward, watching Frances's pixie face light with excitement. "We'll call it the 'Every Little Bit Counts Scrap Drive.'"

Frances whispered it to herself. "I think it's good," she said, meeting Josie's eyes.

"It's clever," Josie said. "And it's true."

Frances grinned. "You're so modest. I mean, after all, you thought of it, so who are you calling clever?"

Josie blushed again. "Do you think it would work?"

Frances nodded. "I think so." She got a tablet from her desk and flipped open the top page.

Josie started thinking. "We need a place to put the scrap, a way to weigh it to see how much we have collected—"

"Where do we send it once we have it all in boxes?" Frances asked abruptly.

Josie had to admit she didn't know. "But we can find out," she said firmly.

Frances was smiling. "Let's make a list of everything we have to find out, then see if we still think we can manage."

Josie reached out and took the tablet from her. Whenever they had to organize a project and make lists, she did it. Her handwriting was much better than Frances's.

"We would have to make posters and signs," Frances said.

"And decide on a final date for donations," Josie added, writing fast.

"We need a place for the scrap to be stored," Frances said thoughtfully.

Josie nodded. "Somewhere in town so that people who come in from Deep Creek or East Cove or somewhere else could just drop it off. They all come into town to go to shop at least once a week."

"The Boy Scouts went and picked up the scrap, didn't they?" Josie mused.

Frances nodded. "Yes. My mother gave them some old aluminum cook pots, and I remember them coming here to get them. Mr. West was with them."

"Maybe he would sponsor a prize, too," Josie said. "West's Grocery is one of the most important businesses in this town. They aren't going to want to be left out of all this."

Frances laughed. "You would make a good press agent, Josie."

Josie kept writing, feeling better every second. Maybe they could do something important after all. Maybe people would see that she was trying to help win the war, even if Tom wouldn't go into the service.

"What else?" Frances asked breathlessly once the list had filled up three pages.

Josie read the entries aloud, then shook her head. "I can't think of anything more. Can you?"

Frances shook her head and smoothed her purple robe. "Do you want to go swimming and then come back and work on the ideas some more?"

Josie laid the tablet aside. "Can I borrow your old suit?"

Frances smiled. "Of course. I pulled it out of every rubber-drive box Mama filled this spring because I knew you'd need it this summer."

Josie stood up and went to the window. It would be a perfect day to swim. The sun was bright, and by the time Frances actually got ready to go, it would be hot.

A movement in the street below caught her eye. She stared for a few seconds without recognizing her brother. Once she did, she leaned forward to press her face against the glass. What was Tom doing in town when he was supposed to be finishing up the combine today? She watched as he rounded a corner and was gone from sight. Josie frowned, her high spirits sinking again.

"What's wrong?" Frances asked, touching her shoulder. "You look upset."

"I'm fine," Josie said quickly. She didn't care what Tom was doing. She was not going to let him ruin *everything* for her.

CHAPTER FOUR

Walking down H Street toward Main, Josie tried to listen to what Frances was saying, but she couldn't stop glancing around. Tom had come this way, too, until she had lost sight of him out the window. She didn't think he would be going to the plunge. It was full of little kids this summer—and their shrill voices and giggles irritated Tom as much as they bothered her.

It seemed like only the little kids were swimming much this summer. Most of the young teenage kids were either helping their parents or working—and the older boys had all gone into the service. The high school girls were busy at home tending Victory Gardens, sewing lap robes for the military hospitals, and writing letters to their favorite soldiers.

Josie sighed.

"What's wrong with you, today?" Frances asked, swinging her pocketbook back and forth. Josie could see a sliver of her bright pink swimsuit poking out. The older, faded blue one was folded below it.

"Nothing," Josie said after a moment. Then she looked aside.

"I don't believe you," Frances said evenly. "Something has been bothering you since you got here."

They stepped off the curb to cross the street, then back up, in perfect unison. Their strides were the exact same length, Josie knew. They had read an article about what it took to get soldiers to march in perfect time and they had practiced all last summer, carrying broomsticks over their shoulders when no one could see them and tease them about acting like boys.

"Maybe my father would buy a war bond and we could give it away to whoever brings in the most scrap metal," Frances said suddenly, scattering Josie's thoughts.

She looked up from the sidewalk, grateful that the subject had changed. "Would he do that?"

"He might. Or maybe he could get Williamson's to sponsor the bond. They could use it in an ad for the store." She tilted her head like a girl in a Sunday paper advertisement. "Williamson's buys its share of war bonds," she said in a perfectly modulated voice. "We are in the forefront of war effort contests and giveaways. Are you contributing the ten percent Uncle Sam needs from every American who can afford it?"

Josie laughed aloud. Frances could imitate the

radio announcers perfectly. If her voice had been deep, like a man's, she could have gotten a job at it, Josie was sure.

"What do you think of the idea?" Frances asked, then hopped over a wide crack in the sidewalk.

Josie followed her. "That would be terrific." Looking down to clear the crack, she noticed that her shoes looked scuffed. Glancing sideways, she saw that Frances's were new and shiny, as always. She kicked at the sidewalk, sliding her foot along, upset that her shoes were old, that her mother hadn't had enough money when the coupons were issued.

"Daddy can probably talk them into it," Frances was saying. "Williamson's could use a community project right now. They want everyone to accept the new OPA decisions."

Josie waited, already half annoyed. She knew that Frances would explain—probably at length. If she didn't grow up to be a writer, she would probably end up being a teacher.

"Do you know about the—"

"The Office of Price Administration," Josie interrupted, annoyed now. "They decide what everything should cost."

Frances just nodded and smiled, ignoring Josie's irritation. "Remember that meeting I told you about last week?" she went on.

"It was in the paper, Frances," Josie said. "And

besides, that's where Mr. Brand was going when he took Mama to Spokane."

Frances arched her brows upward. "I forgot she went with him. Well, the dry goods sellers met here while the grocers and dairymen all went up to Spokane."

Josie stepped over another crack in the sidewalk, then looked at Frances. She was walking along with her head held high, her posture perfect, as always. The hem of her skirt belled out with every step, and the curls in her hair bounced in rhythm. If the war ever ended, and the young men came home, every one of them was going to notice Frances. She would have dates coming out of her ears.

Frances caught Josie watching her and laughed. "What are you thinking about, so dark and deep?"

"That when we are sixteen, you will have hundreds of dates and I will be sitting home alone," Josie said truthfully.

Frances laughed again. "Don't be silly."

Josie looked straight ahead again, and they walked a little ways in silence. Then, as she often did, Frances went right back to what she had been saying before Josie had interrupted her thoughts. "When my father came home, I overheard him telling Mother that the rationing system had been well thought out— that it ought to work."

Josie nodded tentatively, then smiled. Frances

wasn't sounding so much like a teacher now; she just sounded grown up and like she expected Josie to be grown up, too. "My father thinks the OPA men have done a good job with the farm prices so far," Josie said carefully, trying to make her voice even and firm, like Frances's.

Frances lifted her brows. "Our fathers agree for once!"

Josie laughed. Usually, they didn't agree. Her father was a Democrat. Mr. Keener was a party-line Republican.

"Anyway, I'll ask my father this evening," Frances said again.

"If we could have a prize, more people might bring in scrap," Frances was saying as they stepped off the curb to cross Whitman Street. She flounced her skirt. "And the newspaper would print the winner. That would be good for any business. Community recognition."

Josie smiled. It sounded grand the way Frances put it. "It ought to work," she said aloud.

"Oh, look, there's your brother," Frances said suddenly, pointing, as they rounded the corner onto Main Street.

Josie looked, shading her eyes. It was Tom. As she watched, he stopped in front of the Congress Theater and stood, reading the posters out front. Then he walked on.

Josie stared. Why wasn't he home working on the combine? If the weather held, they would be harvesting in a week or two, Daddy had said. Frances walked faster, and Josie lagged. Once they were in front of the theater—with Tom still nearly a block ahead—Josie stopped and stood staring at the posters.

"Why are you frowning like that?" Frances asked, breaking into Josie's thoughts again.

Josie glanced at her. "No reason, I—"

"You look upset," Frances said, concern in her voice. "Is something wrong?"

Josie shook her head, but couldn't keep from staring down the block. Tom was still ambling along, his shoulders drooping, his step lazy and slow. Frances followed her gaze. "Is it something about Tom?"

Josie shook her head quickly. "No, of course not. Nothing at all is wrong with him except Evelyn breaking it off with him and everything."

Frances was examining her face intently, and Josie glanced aside. She made a point of reading the movie posters, hoping that Frances would let it go.

"What is it, then?" Frances insisted. "You *are* upset about something, Josie. I know you."

Josie considered telling her the truth about how oddly Tom was acting, but she didn't want to. Frances was still staring at her, waiting. "We had a robbery last night," Josie said impulsively.

Frances's eyes widened. "A robbery? You mean someone came into your house and—"

"No, not in the house," Josie interrupted. She began to explain, carefully leaving out anything about Tom. Frances listened intently, an expression of astonishment on her face.

"But you have to keep it a secret," Josie pleaded. "Daddy asked me not to tell everyone I met. You know how he is about things."

Frances nodded. "He hates other people in his business."

"Promise you won't tell," Josie pleaded.

"I won't tell a soul," Frances promised. She nodded solemnly, then pretended to lock her mouth shut, twisting an invisible key. Then she tossed the make-believe key into the bushes in Mrs. Alber's yard. Frances started walking again, and Josie followed her down the sidewalk, angry with herself. Daddy had asked her not to tell anyone.

They stepped off the curb together to cross Sumner Street. Frances glanced at Josie, obviously waiting for her to say something.

Josie shook her head. "I don't know why they picked the Buick trunk. I didn't think about it. We were *in* the house. I suppose they could see that." She shivered, imagining someone standing in their yard, peering into her lit window. "They took an old tent of my grandfather's and a five-gallon can of gasoline."

Frances tilted her head. "Well, we all know there are some people who would buy gasoline on the sly if someone had it to sell. And the tent makes sense, if it was hoboes."

Josie shrugged again. "Daddy was furious. That old tent belonged to his father."

Frances didn't answer, and Josie could tell she was deep in thought. Josie found herself staring at the front windows of Williamson's as they came toward it. Frances followed her glance. "I'll ask my father this evening what he thinks about donating a war bond for a prize."

Josie smiled. "I hope he thinks it's a good idea."

"Let's go out to your house," Frances said.

Josie was startled. Frances almost always preferred walking around in town whenever they had time together. "Why?"

France's eyes were sparkling. "Maybe we could solve the crime."

Josie shook her head. "Sheriff Parnell has been out there by now. And my father and Tom already looked at everything there was to see," Josie began, then she stopped herself. Had they? Tom had acted strangely, and her father had been so upset that they both might have missed any kind of evidence. Now that she thought about it, she wasn't even sure if Sheriff Parnell had come out to take a look around. Maybe the phone call had been Sheriff Parnell, asking

Daddy to come into town to write a full report so he wouldn't have to come all the way out to the farm.

Frances was staring at her. "But maybe we could find some little thing that would solve the whole crime. Like in the movies."

Josie looked down the block toward the library. Tom was staring up at the building, his head tipped back so far that his whole body was angled backward. Then he happened to look her way, and Josie could tell that seeing her startled him.

"Hey, Tom!" Frances called, waving. Then she turned toward Josie. "Let's ask him what Sheriff Parnell said."

Josie nodded and lengthened her step to keep up. As the distance between them closed, Josie could see the unfamiliar, tense look was still on Tom's face. His lips were pressed together in the uncomfortable little half-smile she had noticed at breakfast. He looked angry. At what? Her? Josie swallowed hard, wishing her brother would stop acting like a stranger.

CHAPTER FIVE

"What are you doing, Tom?" Frances called out as they crossed Beach Street. She was smiling, and walking so fast that Josie could barely keep up.

Tom had jerked around at the sound of Frances's voice. Now he lifted his right hand to shade his eyes. For the first time, Josie noticed that he was carrying a lunch bag. It swung back and forth, dangling from his left hand as he waited for them to come toward him. Abruptly, he seemed to notice it, too, and shoved it into his back pocket. He glanced up, and his eyes skimmed across Josie's face without really seeing her as he turned and scanned the other side of the street.

Josie frowned. He hadn't come to breakfast, so now he had to carry food around like a schoolboy? And it embarrassed him enough to squash his piece of pie rather than have his little sister notice that he had swiped it from the kitchen? Josie shook her head, angry with him. The bag would probably leak, and the cherry filling would stain his trousers. And she knew she would be the one who would have to try to wash the stains out.

"Tom? What are you looking at?" Frances shouted.

Josie marveled at her friend. Tom looked like a deer about to bound off, his face tense and white, but Frances seemed not to notice anything was wrong. She just strode forward, stepping along the sidewalk like she owned the whole town.

Josie dropped back a half-step, studying her brother as he glanced back at the library, then toward them again. Frances's pace was so quick that Josie had to run a few steps to keep from being left behind, but she watched as Tom shifted his weight from one foot to the other. When they were close enough, he gave them a lopsided smile.

"I just came into town to get a few things," he said, then glanced across the street again. Josie followed his gaze, but there was nothing there except Mr. West and his wife walking down the sidewalk. She waved at them, and Tom called out a polite greeting. Frances smiled and nodded.

"Josie told me about the robbery," Frances said, once the Wests were past. Her voice was breathless, excited.

Josie shot Frances a hard look, but she didn't notice. She was looking into Tom's face so intently that he turned to face her again. "What happened exactly?" she asked him.

"Nothing, really. Someone just broke into the Buick trunk," Tom said in a low, even voice, as though the topic bored him to tears.

"I already told her everything," Josie put in, thinking he was upset about having to explain all about the robbery. But her attempt at letting Tom off the hook with Frances only earned her a fierce look from her brother. She glared at him. He was so touchy and unpredictable lately. No matter what she said or did, it was wrong.

"You have to admit it was pretty strange," Frances said.

"There wasn't anything strange about it," Tom told her. Then he gestured back up the block toward the movie theater. "The posters at the Congress are this week's new ones," he added, and it was obvious he was trying to change the subject. "It's *Underground Agent*, with Bruce Bennet and Leslie Brooks, this week."

"We saw it as we came past," Josie put in, trying to help him out again.

"It's that one and *She Has What It Takes*, with Jinx Falkenburg and Tom Neal," Tom added. Then he started to step around them.

"Tom?" Frances caught his sleeve, arching her eyebrows in such a perfect expression of fascinated curiosity that she looked like a girl reporter in a movie. "Josie said the thieves took a tent and some gasoline!"

Tom nodded. "Among other things."

Josie waited until Tom glanced past Frances and met her eyes. Then she spoke up. "What other things?"

He shrugged. "Daddy remembered there had been some fencing tools in the trunk, maybe an ax from the last fishing trip he took with Mr. Hanson."

Josie stared at him. His face was strained again. "I have to get going," he said abruptly, taking one step backward to free himself from Frances's hand on his shirt. Then he walked forward, and she had to step to one side to let him go past.

"What's wrong with *him?*" Frances demanded in a whisper once Tom was too far away to hear. Then she nodded knowingly. "Phil Bass is going into the service now, too. Isn't he?" Frances turned to look at Josie.

Josie pushed her hair back off her forehead. "Yes."

Frances shrugged. "Poor Tom. Once Phil leaves, both his best friends will be gone. And you said Evelyn had stopped seeing him. I guess I'd feel pretty bad, too."

Josie stared at Frances. "What do you mean?"

Frances made a vague gesture with one hand. "I mean, well, I would feel bad if I were a man and I didn't . . . " She trailed off and cleared her throat. Then she started over. "I just think I would be upset if I wasn't going to fight when everyone else . . . "

Frances's voice faded again, and Josie turned to watch her brother cross Beach Street and glance back. He touched his hand against his back pocket, and she wondered if the bag was leaking yet. Then, he turned the corner and disappeared from sight. "Let's go swimming," she said aloud, resolved to get away from the awkward subject of Tom enlisting.

"All right," Frances said quickly, and Josie could tell she was also relieved to have something else to talk about.

Josie started off, and Frances skip-stepped to catch up. "We have to plan the scrap metal drive, too," Josie reminded her. "Maybe we should just go back to your house after we swim and—"

"I think trying to solve the robbery is a lot more exciting than planning a metal drive," Frances said, cutting her off with a smile. "And, besides, we can do the planning anytime."

Josie didn't answer, her thoughts churning. Frances's brothers—and her parents—were doing so much for the war effort that Frances was already losing interest?! A little angry, and knowing that if she opened her mouth she might say things she would regret, Josie kept up her pace as they made their way along the sidewalk. Her thoughts were circling again.

Maybe Frances wasn't going to help much when it got down to the real work. If not, Josie would just do it alone. She wanted everyone to be astonished at how much scrap they managed to get people to bring. She wanted everyone to be *astounded!*

Twenty years from now, Josie wanted them to say, "Maybe Tom didn't enlist when he should have, but that Poe family really put their shoulders to the wheel and worked for the war effort. Remember that scrap drive?"

Josie sighed. People would remember the soldiers who had risked their lives and the people who had done great things on the home front. They would remember her cousin's friend down in Portland, Jimmy Hargis. He had collected more newspapers than anyone in the whole state, and his picture had been in the newspaper. But there had been dozens of scrap drives, and no one was going to think one more mediocre one was anything special. Unless she somehow figured out a way to make it the best one ever.

Josie sighed again as they crossed Mary Street, retracing the route she and her father had driven coming into town.

Frances turned. "What's wrong?"

"I just want people to know that my family was part of the war effort."

"Everyone is," Frances said firmly. "All the posters say that, and it's true. Everyone has to do their share. Every single person."

Josie didn't answer. Frances couldn't possibly

understand. Her father bought a war bond every single month, and her mother headed three committees in three different clubs that all had war support projects going on all the time. Her brother Jack was working in a munitions factory in Spokane, but most of all, Jim was fighting now in Europe.

"You and your mother rolled bandages," Frances said.

Josie glanced across the street toward the river. She could just see the footbridge and the old school on the other side. "Anyone can roll bandages. That isn't hard."

Frances made a small sound of impatience. "It has to be done, doesn't it? And your mother knitted lap robes for the wounded last winter, and you helped."

Josie shrugged, trying to stop grousing. She knew that if she kept it up, Frances would get irritated. She was almost never in a bad mood herself, and had little tolerance for it in other people.

"And you and your mother can almost all your own fruit and vegetables, don't you?" Frances asked, ignoring Josie's silence.

"We canned beans last week and pickled cucumbers," Josie said slowly. "But everyone does that."

Frances glanced at her as they made their way across Bridge Street. "But, see? You do as much as anyone does. And the scrap drive will be wonderful. I bet my father can talk Williamson's into buying a war bond."

Josie nodded agreeably, hoping that she could fool Frances into dropping the topic. If Mr. Keener could get them a war bond for a prize, that would be wonderful—and she hoped that he would. But it wouldn't add anything to her own family's contribution to the war. It would only mean that in addition to having her brother in danger on the front lines in Europe, Frances's family was working harder than most at home for the war effort.

"Your mother saves all the cooking fat, doesn't she?" Frances said abruptly, interrupting her thoughts.

"Yes," Josie answered, keeping her voice steady even though she felt like screaming. It was true. Mama took their cooking fat into the butcher's every ten days or so. That was about how long it took them to save the thirty-two tablespoons that made up a pound. Mama poured it into clean cans with wide mouths—exactly the way the posters said it should be done. But so what? Everyone knew that the fats were made into explosives, and since most families had sent boys to be soldiers . . . of course they saved fats. Few families would dare hoard anything needed for the war. Their friends and relatives would never forgive them. *Their* sons' lives might depend upon it. Josie sighed. Frances didn't understand. And she never would. Jim was fighting.

Josie wished for the twentieth time that she was old enough to join the Wacs. Then at least she could really do something about the war. There were women pilots flying supplies all over the place, Mama said. Women had taken over air controller jobs, too, and lots of other jobs that there weren't enough men to fill. Josie kicked at a pebble on the sidewalk. She wondered how old you had to be before you could apply for jobs like that. Older than thirteen, that much was sure.

"Oh, no, I can hear them from here," Frances said, pointing with her pocketbook in one hand. The grown-up gesture irritated Josie a little, and it took her a second to come out of her thoughts and understand what Frances was talking about. When she did, she frowned. There was a riot of thin, giggling shrieks and screams coming from the direction of the plunge.

Josie shook her head. "Let's wait until we get over by the gate before we decide." She pushed her hair back off her forehead and veered across the street, Frances following her again. She really did want to swim. And she didn't want to spend the day back at home, even if Frances thought a car trunk robbery was the most fascinating thing she had ever heard of.

Besides, Josie knew that if they went back out

this early, Daddy would think of something for her to do—some chore. All she had done since Mama had left was chores and more chores.

"Josie?" Frances was saying from behind her. "Josie, look."

Josie slowed—and as much as she didn't want to, she had to nod. The plunge was packed this morning, and most of the kids in the pool were little. The noise of the shouts and squeals was nearly deafening, even from here.

Exasperated, Josie turned away from Frances, staring down the Burlington Northern Railroad tracks that ran along the edge of town, parallel to Division Street. That was exactly where she did not want to be in a few minutes—walking along between the tracks and the road, headed home.

"Josie, we can swim any old time," Frances was saying.

"I can't," Josie said so quietly that her whisper was lost in the noise of the kids playing in the swimming pool. She stood very still, trying to think of something else in town that Frances would want to go do. The theater wasn't open yet. They could go to the Oasis, but she didn't have much money to spend, and she didn't like it when Francis paid her way.

As Josie stared down the tracks, her grumpy thoughts drowning out the screaming kids, she was startled to see Tom step out from behind the Grange building on Mill Street. As she watched, he dodged across the road, looking in both directions as he went. He was only visible for a few seconds before he disappeared down Whitman Street, but she was sure it was Tom again—and she was pretty sure of something else. He had been carrying something. It had looked like a gas can.

Josie squinted, as though she could somehow make Tom reappear so she could get a better look at him. It made no sense at all. If Daddy had needed gasoline, he would have gotten it himself when he'd taken her to Frances's. No one made extra trips to town now—not with the war shortages on tires and gas.

Josie glanced back at Frances. She was going through her pocketbook, looking for something. Josie watched for a second, then looked back up the tracks, thinking furiously. Farmers got more gas rationed to them than other people, and Frances was right: Some people would always be dishonest enough to buy illegal, black-market gasoline. If Tom decided to take a few gallons from the machine shed tank, Daddy might not notice.

Josie held very still, hoping some other explanation would pop into her mind, but it didn't. She felt sick. Not only was her brother not going to war like all the other guys his age, it looked like he might be involved in something terrible.

"Maybe it wasn't a gas can," Josie whispered to herself. She felt better, instantly. Maybe it wasn't. What had she seen, really? Just a vague shape, nothing more.

CHAPTER SIX

Josie turned away from Frances while she gathered her wits. All of a sudden, she wasn't sure she wanted to stay in town another minute. If Tom was involved in something terrible like stealing gasoline and reselling it, she couldn't stop him. But she sure as heck didn't want to watch him go about his business. And she knew she should tell Daddy, if she was sure. She clenched her fists. But she wasn't sure. She couldn't bring herself to believe that Tom would do something like that.

"What are you looking at now?" Frances asked.

"Nothing," Josie said, keeping her voice even. She felt funny fibbing to Frances, but she wasn't sure there was anything wrong. Maybe there wasn't. She wanted to believe that.

"Let's just go out to your place," Frances said. "We can plan the scrap drive out there, and I can avoid my mother's Xenodican Club meeting this afternoon. And we can look around for clues about the—"

"All right, let's go, then," Josie said, cutting Frances off midsentence.

Frances's eyes widened. "I know you think it's silly, but I—"

"No, I don't," Josie said, interrupting her again. "And while you play Detective Dotty, I can think about the scrap drive."

Frances laughed. "Detective Dotty. Sounds like a comic strip."

"Do you need to go back by your house?" Josie asked to be polite, knowing that if Frances said yes, she would try to talk her out of it. She did not want to cross paths with her brother again.

Frances smiled again. "No, we can just go from here. I'll call Mama from your house and let her know where I am."

"She won't get upset with you?" Josie asked, but she was already walking, starting across Main Street.

"Slow down a little, Josie," Frances said from behind her. "Now you're in such a hurry, you're practically running!"

Josie glanced back and forced a smile. "I know, I know. But if we aren't going to swim, I may as well get some thinking done while you sleuth around."

"But you have to help me look for clues," Frances said, running a few steps to catch up, then falling into her long stride beside Josie. "Hey," she said suddenly, "I forgot to ask about your aunt Lila."

"Mama said she is doing much better now," Josie answered.

"I am very glad to hear that," Frances said, sounding like an older woman, her voice modulated like her mother's always was. Josie thanked her for her concern, imitating her own mother as she spoke in her own best grown-up voice. Then she giggled.

Frances laughed, too. "So your mother will be coming home, soon?"

"Tuesday," Josie said, letting her voice return to normal. "And I can't wait. I don't know how Mama stands all the work she does in a day. I can't even get it done before it's time to start over."

As they stepped off the curb to cross Whitman Street, Josie glanced around, trying to see as far up the block as she could. Tom had apparently taken off in some other direction.

"You're acting funny today," Frances said. "I guess the robbery must have upset you."

Josie turned to face her. "A little, I guess." Frances looked sympathetic and kept staring at her, so Josie forced herself to look straight northward along Division Street. There was no one else walking today, and as usual, no cars.

Daddy had told her the month before that the inspectors were getting harder on people who went over the thirty-five-mile-an-hour speed limit, braked suddenly, and went around curves too fast. Anyone who wore out tires faster than people who followed the recommendations from the government was out of luck at inspection time. No one could buy new tires without approval. Rubber was way too important to the military to let anyone waste even a little.

"It's hot," Frances said, breaking into Josie's thoughts as they started up the Division Street hill. "We should have gotten a cola at the Oasis or something."

"Or a Green River," Josie said wistfully, wishing she could go. She loved the tall, icy, lime soda. She didn't get to drink it very often.

"Look," Frances said, pointing.

Josie followed her gesture up the hill that rose above Division Street. She couldn't see anything. "What was it?"

Frances didn't answer. Her face was a little flushed. "I thought I saw someone out in the wheat."

Josie shook her head. "No one would cut across like that."

"Maybe it was one of the hoboes," Frances said suddenly, her eyes widening. "They wouldn't care if they ruined someone's wheat, would they?"

Josie looked up the hillside. "Maybe not. But hoboes aren't stupid, Frances. They don't want everyone mad at them."

"But the ones who broke into your father's Buick wouldn't care about that at all, would they?" She shook her head, then kicked at a piece of gravel.

Josie had to admit that it made sense. "I guess not. I mean, if they stole—"

"Exactly," Frances interrupted.

Josie stepped up her pace, partly to stop the conversation from going any further. She was sick of worrying about hoboes and everything else.

"If we hurry, maybe we can see the man again from the top of the hill," Frances said.

Josie nodded. She didn't care about seeing some old hobo cutting across a wheat field, but she didn't mind hurrying. When they walked fast, it was harder to talk and easier to think. She went a little faster, and Frances kept up.

Near the top of the hill, Frances reached out and tugged at Josie's dress. "There!" she said between breaths. "There he is again. Look, Josie!"

Josie turned, scanning the wheat fields they had passed. From here, she could see both sides of the low, rounded hill closest to the road. At first, she thought that Frances was teasing her, or imagining things, but then she saw the distant figure for herself.

It was a man, Josie thought, though it was impossible to see any more detail at this distance. He could have been old or young, tall or short, blond or dark haired. All she could tell from here is that he was walking straight across a wheat field, apparently without a care in the world for the farmer's hard work and the nearness of the harvest.

"That's incredible," Frances whispered. "What must he be thinking?" In spite of all her earlier certainty, she sounded completely amazed now, and Josie understood her perfectly. It was almost impossible to believe that someone could simply trample the wheat and not care.

"We should call Sheriff Parnell," Frances said, glancing at Josie. "That's trespassing, if nothing else."

"Maybe." Josie met her eyes, and when she looked back, the figure was gone. He had either stopped to rest and was hidden by the high wheat, or he had walked into a low area that hid him from sight.

Josie started walking again, following the train tracks, heading for home. She followed the rail riders' path along the Burlington Northern tracks as far as she could, staying just clear of the ends of the ties. She could hear Frances behind her, her shoes crunching on the gravel of the rail bed.

Every few seconds, Josie glanced up at the hills again, expecting to see the man walking. But he did not appear. The rolling hills were empty of everything but tall, yellowing wheat, as far as she could see.

"Look," Frances said quietly. "See the breeze moving through it? Looks like the ocean, doesn't it?"

Josie didn't answer. If Frances stopped to think for even a second, she wouldn't ask such silly questions.

She knew perfectly well that Josie had never been to the ocean.

"Do you see him again?" Frances asked from beside her. "You're staring."

"No," Josie told her, her stomach feeling tight. "I was just thinking."

Frances ran two steps to walk beside her again. "About what?"

Josie took a deep breath. "I want to see the ocean someday."

Frances looked startled, then apologetic. "I've only seen it twice. I barely remember the first time, but the second, we were there all day. It was so beautiful." She said the final word as though she were naming one of the great treasures of the earth. "I wrote you postcards, remember?"

Josie nodded. "Fifth grade, just before Pearl Harbor was bombed. I was so afraid you wouldn't make it home. I thought they were going to bomb us next."

Frances looked sad. "We came home early because of the bombing. It seems like that happened a long, long time ago."

Josie looked away, nodding, suddenly feeling strange. It seemed like the war had been going on forever.

As they topped the rise and started around the bend, Frances pointed behind them. "Look. There's Sheriff Parnell."

Josie shaded her eyes against the bright sun and nodded. It was. Was he coming back from her house? He was driving cautiously down the hill toward town, and it looked like he was peering out the window of his car. When he got closer, Frances clutched her pocketbook under one arm and waved.

"What are you doing?" Josie demanded, startled.

"I'm going to flag him down," Frances said over her shoulder. "I think we should tell him about the man in the wheat field."

Josie could only watch as Frances ran toward Sheriff Parnell's car. The tight, unhappy feeling in her stomach blossomed and spread to include her heart, and she admitted to herself, finally, where it was coming from. The man in the wheat field had been wearing light trousers and a dark jacket. For an instant, when Frances had first pointed him out, she had thought that it might be Tom.

Josie tried to quiet her thudding heart as Sheriff Parnell's car slowed, then stopped. It could not have been Tom. Her brother would never walk through someone else's field. Or would he?

CHAPTER SEVEN

Sheriff Parnell leaned down to look out his car window as Frances pointed across the road. He nodded, and Josie could see his lips moving as he asked Frances a question. Frances answered, pushing her hair out of her face when the breeze ruffled it, shading her eyes.

"Josie?" Frances called suddenly.

Josie stiffened, startled. She hesitated, glancing involuntarily at the hills on the other side of Division Street.

"Come here!" Frances was motioning urgently.

Still reluctant, Josie walked toward the car. "Hello, Mr. Parnell," she said automatically, remembering her manners even though her heart was thudding inside her chest.

"You're someone I wanted to talk to this morning," he said, smiling in a friendly way.

Josie nodded. "Daddy brought me into town."

Sheriff Parnell nodded. "I know. I got out there

a few minutes after he got back. I just have a few questions, Josie," he added, and she nodded.

"Did you see or hear anything unusual that you think might have had something to do with the robbery?" He said it in a clear, measured voice.

She thought about it, trying to be honest with herself, with him. "No," she said finally. And she pulled in a deep breath, knowing it was true. Tom might have been trying to hide something, or get the tent and the gasoline back from the hoboes himself, or something she couldn't figure out yet, but he hadn't had anything to do with the robbery.

"Your father says a gas can is missing, along with the tools and the tent," Sheriff Parnell was saying.

Josie felt her stomach tighten another notch. She had forgotten, but he was right. She tried to picture Tom on Mill Street. She had thought it was a gas can, then dismissed it.

"Are you all right?" Sheriff Parnell asked, looking up at her.

Josie swallowed hard. "Sure," she stammered. "It's a little hot."

"Your face is pretty flushed," Sheriff Parnell said. "Do you girls want a ride back out there?"

"We'd be most grateful," Frances said before Josie could gather her wits to refuse.

"Get on in the back, then," Sheriff Parnell said in his deep, cordial voice. "It's pretty hot to walk today."

Josie stepped back as Frances opened the rear door of the car and climbed in. She followed, inhaling the smell of stale cigarette smoke. She slid into the steep-backed seat and leaned out to catch hold of the door handle. She pulled it shut, then glanced up to see Sheriff Parnell looking over his seat at her.

"You feel all right now?"

Josie nodded and was relieved when he turned to face front again. He ground the gearshift forward, and the car lurched into motion. Slowly, the engine almost idling, he backed up onto the shoulder of the road. Braking, he stopped, then put the car into first gear and eased forward, looking both ways as he cut a tight turn.

"This was lucky!" Frances whispered, smiling.

Josie nodded. "Sure was." She did her best to smile.

Frances settled back into the seat as the car started forward, heading back up the hill. She looked positively blissful.

"You girls just out for a walk today?" Sheriff Parnell asked.

"Sort of," Frances told him. "We're planning a scrap metal drive."

Josie sat up straighter. She really hadn't wanted to tell anyone until they'd gotten further along. She frowned, and Frances glanced at her in time to see her expression.

"It's Josie's project, really," Frances said quickly. Josie looked aside. Making sure she got credit for the idea was the last thing on Josie's mind.

"A scrap drive sounds like a great project, Josie," Sheriff Parnell said politely as he wheeled the car around the last curve and stuck his arm out the window to signal for the turn. "The next war loan bond issue starts in a month or so. That'll get everyone thinking about how to pitch in."

He slowed, maneuvering into the farmyard perfectly, gliding past the mailbox by inches, letting the chickens cluck at the tires as they scuttled to get out of the way.

The instant the car came to a halt, Josie twisted the door handle in a quick arc, pushing on it once she heard the latch click free. "Thanks very much," she said politely to Sheriff Parnell, hoping he wouldn't get out of the car.

"You are most welcome," Sheriff Parnell answered, touching his hat. "Remind your father that I'll be back out this evening. And tell him I forgot to ask him not to touch anything around the old Buick until I can dust for fingerprints this evening."

Josie had already half turned, heading for the house. She stopped. "Fingerprints?"

The sheriff nodded. "I forgot to bring my kit. Usually the prints on anything but a real smooth surface are hard to classify and use. But the chrome on that old car is still pretty shiny, and I thought I could see a couple of prints on it. Probably old ones, but who knows?"

Frances made a little squeal as Josie nodded. "So you'll be coming back for that?"

Sheriff Parnell lifted his hat, then resettled it. "For that, and because I wanted to talk to your brother. We couldn't find him."

"Really?" Josie began, unsure of what she should say. "Well, he's probably in town—"

"You know he is, Josie," Frances interrupted. "We just saw him."

Josie blushed from the roots of her hair to her jawline, amazed and ashamed that she had tried to mislead the sheriff. She wasn't even sure *why* she had done it. Her uneasiness grew, and she could feel her skin radiating heat. "Of course," she said. "We only saw him for a second. I just forgot."

Sheriff Parnell was looking at her intently. "You just saw him in town? Where?"

"In front of the library," Frances said before Josie could answer.

"That's right," Josie added lamely. "By the library."

"We were walking down to the plunge from my house." Frances's voice was bright and perky as it always was.

"Good day to swim," Sheriff Parnell said blandly,

then he looked at Josie. "Remind your father, will you? About me coming back this evening?"

"I will, " Josie told him.

"Keep an eye out for the hobo in the wheat on your way back!" Frances called out as he slid the car into reverse and eased backward. "Maybe he's one of the thieves!"

Sheriff Parnell nodded, an exaggerated motion so Frances could see him through the windshield. Then he ground the gears again and backed out of the drive as deftly as he had pulled in.

"Let's get a soda or something," Frances said as the sheriff's car disappeared back around the bend.

Josie took a deep breath. "I don't know if there is any."

"Oh." Frances looked disappointed.

Abruptly, Josie realized how few times they had actually come to her house in the five years of their friendship. And at Frances's, there was always soda in the refrigerator.

Still uneasy, Josie led the way to the door, opening it and going in without looking back at Frances.

"Tom?" her father called from the kitchen.

"No, Dad, it's me."

"And me, Mr. Poe," Frances said as she followed Josie in.

Josie's father looked surprised when they came

around the corner. "I thought you were going to stay in town awhile."

Josie nodded, completely at a loss for an explanation that would make any sense to anyone, including herself.

"The plunge was crowded with little kids," Frances said into the silence. She was leaning against the doorjamb.

"Will you excuse us, Frances?" Josie's father said. "Maybe you could wait for Josie up in her room?"

"Sure." Frances turned and flounced her skirt once as she started down the hallway. Josie could hear her hesitate at the bottom of the stairs, then start up. She paused again on the landing. Was she trying to listen? Josie glanced at her father. If he knew that Frances had stopped halfway up the stairs, he gave no sign of it.

"Josie? What do you think is going on here?"

Josie stared at her father. His face was grave, serious. She shrugged, unsure of what to say. "I don't know."

He nodded. "That's about how I feel. I can't understand why someone would steal all that stuff out of the old Buick and leave this." He held out a key in the palm of his hand.

Josie recognized it instantly. It was her missing house key. "Where did you find that?"

Her father shrugged. "I didn't. Sheriff Parnell

spotted it in the dust by the Buick. I told him you must have lost it."

Josie nodded. "I did, and I was going to tell you soon, but—"

"But it seemed like enough was going wrong already?"

Josie nodded. "And I guess I was afraid it would make you angry at me."

Daddy was shaking his head. "It probably would have. I don't want you to be careless with it, Josie."

She nodded. "I'm not. Honest. I don't know how in the world I lost it—but I lost it a week ago. And I never, ever go over by that old car."

He nodded. "That's what I was afraid you were going to say."

Josie looked out the window to keep from meeting his eyes. Nothing was making sense. Her father suddenly slapped his palm against the table. "It had to have been hoboes. Nothing else adds up." He pushed his chair back and stood, holding out the key. Josie opened her hand, and he dropped it into her palm. "Hoboes don't explain this, though," he said thoughtfully.

Josie tried to think of some way that her key could have gotten from her room, across the yard, then into the dust beside the Buick. She couldn't.

"Maybe you dropped it in the road on your way home from somewhere, and a crow carried it a ways, then just dropped it by the old Buick. They like shiny things." He shook his head. "As for catching the hoboes, maybe Tom'll know something that will help," he added, ruffling her hair. "You'd best get upstairs before Frances has a curiosity fit."

Josie blushed. "I told her about it a little," she admitted.

Her father frowned, but he nodded. "I knew you would. Did you say anything to anyone else?"

Josie shook her head. "No one."

Daddy smiled. "I just hate the way rumors fly around this little town sometimes."

"I hate all this," Josie said quietly. She hadn't meant to say it, and she wasn't even sure what she'd meant by it.

Her father nodded, anyway. "There's enough wrong in the world without looking for more trouble, isn't there?"

Josie found herself looking into his face. He looked tired and sad, and she knew exactly what he meant. "Mama says the war can't last forever."

He pretended to shoo her, clapping his hands like Mama did when the chickens were in the garden. It was an old game from when she was little, and it made her giggle. As she started up the stairs, she found herself frowning.

Daddy was trying hard not to let the robbery upset him. He was right about one thing: There was enough wrong in the world without looking for more trouble. Josie hesitated on the landing, wishing she knew what Tom was doing. Then she forced herself to stop frowning and went on up the stairs.

CHAPTER EIGHT

"What's the big secret?" Frances demanded as Josie came through the door. She was sitting on the edge of Josie's bed, impatiently brushing the chenille bedspread with her right hand.

Josie shook her head. "Nothing much. Just that he found my house key."

Frances looked disappointed. "Oh. I thought it was something about the robbery. Let's go have a look around."

Josie started to balk, but she saw how excited Frances looked and she couldn't help but smile. "You really ought to be a girl reporter when you grow up."

Frances pouted. "Mother says the same thing. I don't see why you think it's funny. I just like figuring things out."

"Girl detective, then."

Frances blushed. "I think it would be swell to be solving mysteries all day long."

Josie arched her brows. "I don't think anyone

ever really does that. Not all day every day. How could they?"

Frances frowned. "What do you mean? In the cities like Chicago or New York there are all kinds of police detectives and they always try to figure things out."

"I figured something out just now," Josie said, making her face as serious as she could.

"What?" Frances said cautiously.

"That you read far too many dime novels. You're starting to think everything is exciting and mysterious."

"Some things are," Frances insisted, edging toward the door. "Come on. Let's go out and look around. We can always come back in and sit around later when it's too hot to do anything else."

Josie turned reluctantly. "I'm sure there's really nothing to see."

Frances laughed. "Maybe not to the inexperienced eye. But to Frances Keener, girl detective—"

"All right, all right," Josie gave in. It wouldn't hurt to go outside and walk around the farmyard, she supposed. It would keep Frances from getting bored and deciding that she wanted to go back to town after all.

Frances danced down the stairs, and Josie followed her. "Where is it?" Frances asked the instant they had emerged into the sunshine.

Josie pointed. "Over there."

The Buick was parked between the old truck

that didn't run and the rusty, narrow-tined harrow. Neither the Buick nor the truck had tires. They had gone to a rubber drive long ago, even before the new regulations about hoarding tires had been put in place.

Frances clicked her tongue. "Who would even think to look in the trunk of *that?*"

The instant that Frances said it, Josie found herself wondering the same thing. Who would?

Frances had her hands on her hips. "Why would anyone think there was anything of value in there? Why not rob the toolshed or the machine shed or the house?"

Josie shrugged. "How would I know?"

Frances walked forward slowly, as though the old car were something alive and shy—like a colt that she might startle.

Josie caught at her sleeve. "Don't touch anything. Sheriff Parnell said he was going to dust for fingerprints this evening."

"I know that," Frances said, turning to look at Josie over her shoulder.

Josie nodded. "So, don't touch anything."

Frances smiled. "I won't. I can't wait to watch. It's called dactyloscopy. Isn't that a strange word?"

Josie shrugged. "I suppose. There really isn't anything more to see out here, is there?"

Frances looked at the Buick again. "Come on, Josie, this is the scene of the crime! The robbery happened right here. Isn't that even a little interesting to you?"

"You make it seem like we're dealing with some big mystery," Josie said wryly.

Frances looked offended and she started to reach for the door handle.

"Don't!" Josie said loudly.

Frances pulled her hand back before Josie could say another word. "I just forgot," she said defensively, stepping back.

"Some girl detective you'd make," Josie groused. "Come on, let's go back inside and—"

"You're taking this too lightly, Josie," Frances said. "The robbers were right outside your house." She turned back and pointed. "Practically right under your window. Don't you want them arrested?"

Josie sighed. "I don't think they're dangerous, whoever they are. I think Tom is right—it was hoboes." Frances started to respond, but Josie held up one hand to stop her. "And I think we should get to work on a plan for a scrap drive, Frances."

"We will, we will," Frances said. She suddenly turned toward the house. "Oh, I forgot. I should call my mother."

Go ahead," Josie nodded, seizing the chance to look around by herself. "I'll wait for you out here."

"Don't find any evidence until I get back," Frances said.

Her face was somber, but her words sounded so funny Josie almost laughed. Then she looked into Frances's eyes and realized how serious she was. "I won't," Josie said, sure it was true.

Frances spun around and ran for the front door. She hesitated on the front steps and called back across the yard, "This should only take a minute! I'll be right back!"

"Okay," Josie called. Then Frances disappeared into the house. Once she was out of sight, Josie turned to look at the old Buick again, wishing the tireless hunk of metal could talk. "Was Tom out here when the robbery was going on?" she asked it. "Did he talk to the hoboes and feed them dinner first? Or was he just mopey and slouchy like he has been and walked straight past without noticing anything?"

Josie nodded to herself. That was the most likely answer, after all. And Tom was probably reluctant to say that he had been outside because he was ashamed to admit he had been that oblivious to strangers in the yard. Daddy would be upset with him.

"None of which explains the gas can," Josie whispered to herself. She did not believe for an instant that her brother had stolen the gas can from the Buick. But what had Tom been doing? Josie's thoughts were whirling and refusing to make any sense. Why would Tom be getting gas on foot like that? Why wouldn't he wait until Daddy had to come into town for something else and get a ride in? Josie caught her breath.

Maybe Tom was trying to get back in Evelyn's good graces by promising to take her somewhere exciting. Maybe he was sneaking gasoline from town and hiding it on the farm, saving it for a drive to Spokane? If so, Daddy was going to be furious with Tom for using gas coupons without asking—or hoarding gasoline somewhere. Josie had a thought that made her breath catch again. Maybe Tom was *buying* black-market gasoline.

Josie shook her head. He wouldn't do that any more than he would steal gas, she was sure. At least she hoped he wouldn't. If he got caught at it, he would be arrested. Then what would she say to everyone she knew? How could she admit that her brother was not only avoiding the army as long as possible but that he was buying gas that should have gone to the troops overseas? Josie's stomach tightened.

She stared at the old car before her, wondering if the answers to all her questions were somehow right here in front of her—if she could only figure out a way to read them. The Buick's fenders were layered with dust, and there wasn't a mark or print on any of them.

Print, Josie thought abruptly, and froze, staring down at her feet. *Footprints*. There were perfect outlines of flat-heeled shoes in the powdery dust. Hers.

She was sure that Sheriff Parnell hadn't said anything about footprints in the dust. He had only said not to touch anything. But maybe he had meant that they weren't supposed to get close to the Buick at all.

Feeling foolish, Josie stepped backward, bumping into the truck hard enough to lose her balance. Unable to right herself, she sat down on the running board, scraping her leg on the rough, rusty edge. For a few seconds, she just sat still, feeling like crying, even though she knew it was silly. Her leg stung a little, but the scrape was nothing.

A soft clinking sound made Josie look up. It came again, then stopped. Puzzled, she tried to see, but the Buick was in her way. It was probably just the chickens, scratching at something metal. Daddy had old pieces of machinery and chains and old tools everywhere in the yard. "So calm down, girl detective," she whispered to herself, feeling even sillier than she had about the footprints. She was as bad as Frances.

The sound came again, and this time there was a little rhythm to the soft clinking. "Just chickens pecking at something," she said to herself, but she stood and rose to her tiptoes, trying to see what had made the sound.

She couldn't see anything at all except the old harrow and a rusting water tank stacked on the edge of the farmyard by the barbed-wire pasture fence.

Josie sighed. Her own father was holding back scrap that should be on its way to making more guns and tanks.

The soft clinking started up again, and Josie made her way around the Buick, trying to locate the source of the sound. She walked slowly, her head tilted, pausing when it stopped, then going on when it started up again.

She crossed the yard east of the house, wading the high weeds along the fence. She could hear the cows lowing down in the cow barn behind the house and she hesitated, wondering if Tom had remembered to feed them. She shook her head. He was getting careless about some of his chores—and it wasn't fair. He knew he had to feed the cows the same way she knew she had to help Mama do laundry or make supper. Feeding the farm stock was his job, and it had been since he was ten or twelve. It was his *responsibility*. Just like enlisting to help fight the war.

The clinking sound started again, then stopped. Josie looked toward the toolshed. That's where it had to be coming from. There was no other possibility, really. But Daddy was inside, and Tom was still in town, she was pretty sure.

Josie stood rooted for a second, wondering if the hoboes had come back. Or maybe they had never really left. Maybe they were inside the toolshed right now, filling burlap sacks with the rest of her father's pliers and wrenches. Maybe the fencing tools from the Buick trunk had made them decide to come back. Or they had hidden somewhere, waiting for a chance to get more things they could sell to unsuspecting people over in Moscow, across the Idaho line—or down in Spokane.

The idea made Josie furious. Tools were expensive, and new ones were scarce the way things were now, with the war and everything. Josie knew her father probably wouldn't be able to replace them easily, even if he had the extra money to spend—which he didn't.

Stepping forward quickly as the sound began again, Josie doubled over and ran. She ducked around the back of the shed and circled it, the stiff grass scratching at her legs and catching at her skirt. On the back side, she stopped beside the cloudy little window and leaned forward, trying to see inside. She couldn't. The dust on the glass was too thick.

The clinking started up again, and Josie jumped, startled. It was coming from just inside the window. She leaned forward again, rubbing a tiny circle in the bottom corner of the window free of dust.

Crouching down, Josie put her eye close to the murky glass, her heart thudding. She saw a blur of motion, a man's silhouette, which sharpened when a bright rectangle of light suddenly shone into the shed. Then she heard the sound of the door closing on the far side of the shed. Whoever it was had gone out.

Josie straightened up, whirling around. The man would have to cross the yard, or head out across the fields. Either way, if she hurried, she would be able to see him. She slouched low again and ran along the side of the shed, headed back the way she had come. At the end of the building, she paused. If it was the thief, she might be putting herself in danger.

"Josie?"

It was Frances, calling from the front yard. And she would just keep hollering until she got an answer, Josie knew.

"Josie? Where did you go?"

Frances came into sight, and Josie lifted her hands and waved, then put one finger to her lips.

"What are you doing?" Frances yelled, smiling.

Josie shook her head frantically, pointing.

"Josie, my mother says I can stay for supper," Frances said, starting toward her. "Come on, I don't want to play games."

Josie gave up and broke into a run, sprinting toward Frances, gesturing as she ran. "What in the world is wrong with you?" she exploded as she came to a stop.

Frances frowned. "What are you talking about?"

"There was someone in the shed," Josie began. "I was trying to see and I—"

"Someone?" Frances interrupted. "You mean you think the thief is still around?"

Josie nodded, then shook her head. "I don't know," she managed. She was breathing hard, more from being nervous than from the short dash across the yard.

"Oh, well, look," Frances said suddenly, and she sounded so disappointed that Josie knew, before she turned, what she was going to see.

"It's just your brother," Frances scoffed. "Now who's being a misguided girl detective?"

Josie pressed her lips together. Tom waved at them, frowning, an irritated, distracted gesture. Then he walked the other way.

"He must have been right behind us on the way home," Frances said. "I wonder why we didn't see him?"

Josie shrugged, staring after her brother. Maybe he had been the one walking through the wheat after all. On his way home from buying black-market gasoline. Or selling stolen gas. Josie felt a surge of anger and turned aside so Frances wouldn't notice. Why did Tom have to do everything he could to make her even more ashamed that he was her brother?

CHAPTER NINE

For a few seconds, Josie could only stand and watch Tom walk away, his shoulders hunched up as though it were cold out instead of a hot summer day. He stalked across the house yard, past Mama's lilac hedge, then headed toward the machine shed that sat next to the first wheat field. Maybe he was going to go work on the combine.

"Josie!"

Daddy's voice made Josie turn around to face the front door.

"What?"

"Get in here, both of you!" He turned and went back inside.

Frances glanced at Josie as they started toward the house. "He's upset about something."

Josie shrugged. "He sure sounds like it."

"But what did we do?"

Josie could only shake her head unhappily. "Beats me. I already told him you knew about the robbery. Did you say anything to him when you called your mother?"

Frances shook her head. "Nothing. I thought he was outside. I didn't even see him when I went in."

Josie turned to walk up the concrete steps. Frances followed behind her, hanging back a little. Her father was at the hall table, facing the telephone. He turned the crank hard, going around three times before the operator answered.

"Give me Sheriff Parnell's office," he said loudly into the receiver. Then he turned to face Josie. "Go find your brother."

Josie nodded but waited, thinking that he would explain, at least a little. He didn't. After two or three seconds, he frowned at her. "Josie! Find Tom, then get back here, quick."

Josie turned, startled by the harsh tone of his voice. She hurried back out the door, aware that Frances was close behind.

"What's all this about?" Frances asked as they crossed the yard again.

Josie shook her head, her stomach tight. "I have no idea. It scares me, though."

"Do you think something happened with your aunt?" Frances asked.

Josie almost stumbled. That hadn't occurred to her at all. "I don't know," she said aloud. "I hope not." Then she exhaled as her thoughts cleared. "No, it's not Aunt Lila. Daddy wouldn't call Sheriff Parnell about her."

"Maybe it has something to do with the robbery," Frances said, and her voice had the breathless quality that let Josie know she was getting caught up in the mystery again.

"I doubt it," Josie said, just to keep Frances from continuing, trying to figure everything out. She walked faster and turned to follow the path along the east side of the house, walking between the side porch and the toolshed. "Tom is supposed to be cleaning up the combine," she said as they passed the last of the lilac bushes and lawn grass that marked the house yard and crossed into the dust of the farmyard. "Maybe he's actually doing what he is supposed to."

"Hey, wait up," Frances said, running a few steps to keep up.

"Daddy said to hurry," Josie answered without slowing. Then she lifted her chin and cupped her hands around her mouth. "Tom?" she called.

There was no answer. Frances touched her arm. "If he's inside the machine shed, he can't hear you."

Josie nodded to show she had understood, but then she called out again. Tom might be inside working on the combine, but he could just as easily be carrying hay to the horses or the cows, or filling the pigs' mud wallow. Or stacking feed sacks or shoveling manure or untangling the trellis twine Mama had asked him to straighten out. Frances didn't understand about farm chores.

"Tom!" Josie yelled again.

There was still no answer. She led the way up the path and opened the machine shed door. Inside, parked at an angle so that the long blades did not bump the far wall, stood their combine.

"It always looks like a giant insect to me," Frances said from behind her.

Josie nodded again. "It does." Frances had said it before, but it was true. The combine blades stuck out like a lopsided giant pair of pincers, and the sack chute slanted down on the other side like an angled grasshopper's leg.

Josie walked to the far side of the big machine. "Tom?" There was no answer, and she peered into the shadows.

"He isn't in here," Frances said from the doorway.

"Tom?" Josie said once more. It was obvious that Frances was right, but for some reason she had been hoping he would be here, where he was supposed to be, for once. "Let's check the hay shed," she said aloud, coming back around the combine. Tom hadn't even finished cleaning it yet. There was a bristle of last year's wheat straw stuck in the wheel spokes, and there was dirty oil gummed along the rim of the motor housing. Did Daddy know how little Tom had gotten done?

Josie noticed a little corner of brown paper sticking out from beneath the sack chute and, without knowing exactly why, she reached down and tugged at it. As she pulled it free, she saw that it was a small sack. She opened it and looked inside, her breath catching. There were twenty or thirty bullets in it.

"Which one is the hay shed?" Frances asked from the doorway.

"I'll be right there," Josie said, closing the bag and putting it back beneath the sack chute. Then, on impulse, she pulled it free again and shoved it into an old cookie jar on the workbench that Daddy used for gaskets and washers.

"Josie?" Frances called. "What are you doing?"

"Coming," Josie said, walking back toward her. They stepped back out into the sunshine.

Josie pointed toward the back of the three-sided plank structure that shielded the haystack from wind and rain. "Over there. But I don't see him." She started walking, anyway, glancing back and forth across the farmyard as she went. Her mind was working furiously. *What was Tom doing with bullets? Was that what he had put in his pocket in town?*

"But, Josie?" Frances said, following her. "Why would he be in the hay shed, anyway? I thought you said he was supposed to be cleaning up the combine."

Josie shrugged. "He has other chores, too."

Frances frowned. "But you said he was supposed to be here."

Josie nodded vaguely. "Maybe I was wrong." She didn't want to argue about what she had said or not said. Besides, Frances would never get it. She did chores at home, but only easy ones, and her mother gave her a list and she checked each job off as she worked. When she was done, she got to do what she wanted. Farm chores were different. They were endless and they were never done. Frances didn't really understand that, and Josie doubted she ever would.

"But we just saw him," Frances said from behind her.

Josie nodded. "He has to be close." She walked all the way across the farmyard to the hay barn and circled it. He wasn't there. "Tom?" she called, facing the cow barn, then the shed that served their three old mares as a stable. She went past the corral, looking out toward the Victory Garden. Her bean plants were getting tall, and the crop had set. She scanned the edge of the corn rows angling her path until she could see all the way to the road. Tom was not there.

"Where could he have gone that fast?" Frances grumbled.

Josie shook her head. "I don't know. Please stop asking."

Frances looked hurt. "What ever else is wrong, it isn't my fault."

Josie tightened her fists, looking around. "I know that. I'm just upset."

Frances put her hands up to her mouth and began calling Tom's name over and over. Her voice was higher than Josie's, almost shrill, and Josie began to hope it would carry farther, that if Tom had gone out into one of the home-place pastures, he would hear and shout back. But he didn't answer, and she couldn't spot him.

"Maybe we should go tell your father that we can't find him," Frances said finally, lowering her hands and her voice.

Josie nodded, then shook her head. "You go tell him. I'll keep looking."

Frances hesitated. "Or I could keep looking, and you—"

"I know where to look," Josie said, hoping it was true. She knew that Frances didn't want Daddy to shout at her. And he might, the state he was in.

"But, I—" Frances protested.

"Please, Frances," Josie interrupted her again, "just go!"

Frances nodded and turned back toward the house, walking fast. Josie waited until she was back by the machine shed, then she ducked behind the haystack and stood very still, trying to think. If Tom was anywhere close, he had ignored their calls. Would he do that? Josie realized she had no idea what her brother would do. He had hidden bullets and maybe sold or bought gas. He might even have traipsed through someone's wheat without caring how much damage he did.

Josie shook her head. It was as though Tom had become another person—someone she didn't know at all. She looked around the farmyard again. Where would he go? Suddenly, she had an idea. His old hideout.

Josie started walking toward the pasture fence. If he was in one of the barns or the well house, or some-where like that, she could find him on her way back. She broke into a run, glancing back toward the house once or twice. No one was outside, and she hoped no one would appear until she was over the pasture hill and out of sight.

Josie stopped at the fence, bending to gather her skirt close to her legs. The last thing she needed was to tear the yellow rayon on the barbed wire—but the gate was up beside the house, and she didn't want Daddy to see her and ask where she was going.

Placing one hand carefully on the middle strand of wire, Josie pushed it downward, ducking beneath the top wire as she stepped through. Then she hopped free of the wire as she straightened up and released her skirt. Taking a deep breath and glancing back toward the house, Josie kicked off her shoes, then set off across the pasture at a run.

If she was wrong, and she probably was, she didn't want to waste much time following her hunch. Whatever had happened, it was something serious. She wouldn't have much time before Daddy came looking for her.

CHAPTER TEN

The uphill path was sunken, dished out from decades of cows' hooves. Josie ran barefoot beside it, not on it, jumping over manure and clumps of bunchgrass. With every stride, she was acutely aware that from the kitchen window, her bright yellow dress would be impossible to miss. If Daddy happened to look out, he would probably come after her, and Tom would never forgive her for that.

Topping the first rise, Josie forced herself to keep running, following the narrow creek bed that curved along the base of the hill. The sun was glaring in the western sky, hot and blindingly bright on the yellowing wheat. Josie's dress clung to her shoulder blades as she ran, and she could feel a sheen of perspiration on her forehead. The soil here was volcanic sand, dark and gritty, clinging to her bare feet.

By the time she was rounding the corner past the stand of cottonwood trees that hid the rocky hillside beyond, Josie was feeling foolish. What if Tom wasn't here? Her breath heaving, she came to a stop and put her hands around her mouth to shout, "Tom?"

There was no answer, so sound at all. She stood ankle deep in the black sand and listened desperately, but he didn't respond.

"Tom?!" She shrieked his name this time, and her shrill voice came bounding back to her from the rocky hillside beyond the cottonwoods. She walked forward, passing into the welcome shade of the big trees, scanning the hillside. She wasn't quite sure where Tom's old fort was.

The three long-ago times she had seen him coming out of the stand of cottonwoods she had been on the other side of the draw, hiding in the bushes. Every time, she had held her breath—nervous about spying on her big brother. She'd seen him carrying an old blanket once; another time it was a cracked salad bowl Mama had thrown out. Wherever his private retreat was, it was probably pretty well furnished—unless he had taken everything out when he had outgrown the need to have a secret place. Josie frowned. She had been so ashamed of spying on him. Now she wished she had been a better spy.

"Tom? Are you out here? Tom, answer me!" she shouted again.

There was only silence, not even a breeze to rustle the leaves.

"Daddy says to come to the house, quick!" she yelled at the rocky hillside, scanning the bushes and rocks, trying to see the arch of a cave opening or a place where he had built a platform or something into the rocky face of the hillside. She couldn't. "Come back up to the house, Tom," she shouted at the hillside. "Daddy needs us both. Right now!"

After a full minute of silence, Josie clenched her fists, whirling around and running through the gritty black dirt toward the house. As she ran, she lectured herself. Why had she thought that Tom would be in his old fort? What a foolish guess. He was a man now, and she was pretty sure he hadn't spent time up here since his freshman year in high school. It was like expecting her to be in her room playing with her blocks and her stuffed bear.

Josie slowed to run up the last incline, then dropped back to a walk to cross the pasture again, her breath coming hard and fast. The side yard was empty as she tossed her shoes over the barbed-wire fence, then ducked back through. Trying to hurry, she scooped up her shoes and kept going without putting them on. She made her way around the toolshed, glancing at the little circle of rubbed glass on the back window as she went past it.

"Josie!"

She was so startled by the sound of Tom's voice that she jumped. He was standing on the lawn, his hands on his hips.

"Where were you?" she demanded.

"Where have *you* been?" he countered, his eyes straying from her face to the shoes she was carrying.

She frowned. "Looking for you. What's wrong? Did Daddy tell you?"

Tom shook his head. "I didn't know anything was wrong. I just came up from the cow barn."

Josie stared at him. He had been standing by the row of lilacs that marked the edge of the house yard when she had looked up. But the yard had been empty when she'd come through the fence, she was sure. So if he had been in the cow barn, he had to have come all the way around the house, passing the back door on his way.

"You look red as a beet," Tom was saying. "You should get in out of the sun."

Josie looked into his eyes. "Where's Frances?"

"I don't know," he told her, his gaze direct. "You should keep track of your own guests, Josie."

The sarcastic tone of his voice set her teeth on edge. "Daddy sent me out to find you, and you weren't in the machine shed or—"

"I was cleaning out the stalls in the cow barn," he said evenly.

"Daddy wants us both to come in," Josie said, starting toward the front of the house. Tom fell in beside her. Josie walked fast, hoping he wouldn't ask her why she was carrying her shoes, trying to remember if she had yelled Tom's name close enough to the cow barn that he should have heard her. She was pretty sure she had.

"There you are!" Frances called from the front porch as they rounded the corner. She looked frightened, her face pale. "Hurry!" she hissed at them. "Your father is pacing back and forth in the living room, waiting for you."

Josie glanced at Tom as he went up the steps and went past Frances into the hall. "Take your shoes off," she said automatically, sounding like Mama. Flecks of manure got into the carpets, and it was hard to get rid of the barn smell. But Tom either didn't hear her or he ignored her, and she had to run up the steps to catch up to him in the hall.

"It's about time," Daddy exploded as they came in.

"What's wrong?" Josie asked, her heart beating hard. She set her shoes at the foot of the stairs.

"Where in the devil were you?" Daddy demanded, looking at Tom.

Tom shrugged. "Mucking out the barn."

Daddy glared at Josie. "What took you so long to find him, then?"

Josie felt her cheeks flushing. She struggled to think of an answer that wouldn't be a lie but would keep Tom from knowing that she had spied on him when she was little. He would be furious with her, she was sure, even after all this time. "I called and called," she said finally, looking at Frances.

"She called all over the barnyard," Frances affirmed, and Josie shot her a second, grateful look.

"You weren't out there when I went to find you," Daddy said flatly. "Where were you?"

Josie swallowed hard. At that second, the phone rang. Out of long habit, they all stopped talking and listened as the rings came. Three long, then two short. Daddy strode into the hallway. He plucked the receiver out of its cradle and held it to his ear. "Yes," he said. "Yes, it is."

Josie glanced at Tom. He was watching Daddy intently, his face somber. She looked at Frances. "What happened? Did he explain anything to you?"

Frances shook her head. "He said he would wait until you were both here. That was all. He called someone, but I couldn't tell who it was. He asked me to try to find you. He rang the operator when I was on my way out."

Josie moved closer to Frances and pulled her a step or two away from Tom. He didn't seem to notice. His attention was focused down the hallway where Daddy stood, talking quietly into the phone. It was hard to hear what he was saying.

"And when you came out, you couldn't find me?" Josie whispered to Frances.

Frances nodded. "Where did you go? I ran all the way down past the machine shed and—"

"Did you tell Daddy that I wasn't there?"

Frances nodded slowly. "Yes, and he went out and looked while I waited by the phone. Then he came back in and sent me out to look some more. I was on my way when you and Tom came around the corner."

Josie nodded slowly.

"I'll see you in a little while, Pete," Daddy said in a normal voice.

Josie saw Tom shift his weight nervously, but then he smiled thinly. "Is all this about the robbery, then?"

Daddy was coming back up the hall. "More or less. I called Pete to hurry on up and get out here. The thieves took my guns."

Josie caught her breath. "Your deer rifle and —"

"And the shotgun," Daddy said. "Right out of my closet. I was gone for two hours or so in town," he said, his brow furrowing. "Right after I dropped you off, I went over to the Grange to find Tim Hanson. I wanted to check on seed pea prices and a few other things." He looked at Tom.

"I'm not sure when they did it—last night, and I slept through it, or this morning while we were all gone," he said.

"But the door isn't damaged at all," Frances said.

Josie glanced at her. It was true. How could anyone have broken in without leaving marks on the doorjamb?

Daddy was staring at her. "Maybe they used a key."

Tom shrugged again, and his face was a mask of disbelief. "That's impossible. No one has keys but us and—"

"I lost mine a week ago," Josie said miserably. "And Daddy found it out by the old Buick."

Tom turned to stare at her. "What?"

"Her key has been missing a week or more. I found it half covered in dust out there."

Josie shook her head. "I thought maybe it was at the Congress when we went to see that last cowboy show, but I—"

"But who would even know whose door it fit?" Frances said suddenly. "It doesn't make sense."

"If someone saw her drop the key," Tom said quickly, "they could easily ask anyone at the Congress who she was and where we live. Everyone knows us."

Daddy was nodding. "That's all I can figure. Josie, I wish you had been more careful."

Josie felt hot tears stinging at her eyes. Was all of this her fault? "I am careful with my key. I am."

"Half the time you and Mama don't even lock up when you leave," Tom put in.

"We will now," Daddy said. "You can bet on that." He shook his head. "I hate to think what a thief will do with my guns."

Josie leaned against the wall. The plaster felt

cool through her damp dress. The idea of a thief seeing her drop her key, then asking someone where she lived, made her feel almost sick. Who would do something like that? But another idea was scaring her even more. Tom often borrowed Daddy's guns to hunt, or to shoot at coyotes that came too close to the chicken coop. But why would he *hide* bullets?

"So it might not have been hoboes," Daddy said. "Maybe it was someone in town."

"It had to be," Frances said. "And someone will remember a stranger asking about Josie."

Josie shook her head. "How can we ever find out?"

Frances tucked her hair back behind her ears. "Interview everyone. Ask Mr. Byers, who was there that night. He could remember a few, they would remember others. You could put an ad in the *Republican*—everyone would see it, even the people who live way out of town get the paper."

Tom glanced at Frances, then at Josie. "But if no one in town remembers, that doesn't mean much. You could have lost your key anywhere," he said. "In the fields, on your way into town to swim . . . anywhere."

Josie nodded, watching his face intently. "I guess so."

"So whoever found it could have followed you home." Josie nodded.

"What's your point, Tom?" Daddy demanded.

"Just that this might not be as easy to solve as Frances thinks it will be."

"Don't forget dactyloscopy," Frances said suddenly. They all turned to stare at her. Josie pushed away from the wall. She wasn't in the mood to listen to Frances showing off.

"What?" Tom asked.

"Dactyloscopy," Frances repeated. "Fingerprints."

"That's just in the movies," Tom said, laughing.

Daddy was shaking his head. "No, Sheriff Parnell was planning on dusting the Buick for prints this evening. Now that my guns are missing, he's coming right out. He just has to go to Ankcorn's first to get a soft brush for the powder. His old one was moth-eaten."

"Is there any reason for me to stick around the house?" Tom asked abruptly. "Or can I get back to my chores?"

Daddy shrugged. "Go right ahead. Just don't go far. Sheriff Parnell wants to talk to you."

"Why?" Tom asked sharply.

Josie looked at her brother. He shifted his weight from one foot to the other, then back.

"He said they couldn't find you this morning," Josie said to end the uncomfortable silence.

Daddy was looking intently at Tom. "That's right. We couldn't."

"I went up to drive the cows into the hillside

pasture," Tom said evenly. "Then I walked to town to see if I could run in to Evelyn at her aunt's store." He looked sad. Josie felt her heart thudding inside her chest. Maybe all this *was* all about trying to get back with Evelyn. Maybe he wanted enough gas to take her to the Riverside Rolling Rink outside Potlatch, or maybe all the way to Natatorium Park in Spokane. But what did the bullets have to do with anything?

"I saw Josie and Frances by the library," Tom added in the same somber voice.

Josie nodded when her father glanced at her. "We were walking down to swim, but the plunge was so crowded, we gave up on the idea and came out here."

"We got back at almost the same time," Frances said. "We must have just missed each other on Division Street heading out here."

Daddy ran one hand through his hair. "Just stay close until the sheriff comes," he said, glancing from Josie to Tom. Josie nodded. Then Daddy started off down the hall toward the front door.

Frances nudged Josie. She turned. Frances was frowning, making furtive gestures. "Tell him I'm staying," Frances whispered.

"Oh," Josie said aloud, finally understanding. "Daddy?"

He stopped and looked back at her. "What?"

"I invited Frances to supper."

He nodded. "That's fine. Just both of you stay out of Sheriff Parnell's way."

"We will," Frances piped up.

Daddy nodded. "See that you do." He glanced at Josie. "If your mother calls tonight, I want you and Tom to keep all this to yourselves. No reason to worry her."

"All right, Daddy," Josie said.

"Yes, sir," Tom added.

Daddy looked at them both a few seconds longer, then he walked away from them again, turning into his room halfway down the hall. He banged the door closed.

Josie saw Tom flinch at the sound. Then he turned without a word and headed for the back door. She glanced at Frances, then down at the carpet. Tom had left two prints that traced the rims of his shoes.

Josie whirled around, but Tom was already out the door.

"What's wrong?" Frances asked.

Josie pointed. "Manure. How thoughtful of him."

"I'm sure he didn't even notice," Frances said quickly.

Josie stalked away from her, going into the kitchen. She opened the cabinet beneath the sink and pulled out a cleaning rag. She dampened it in the sink and grabbed the dustpan before she went back to the parlor.

"Josie?" Frances said as she got close. "I was just thinking—"

"What?" Josie snapped.

"Don't get mad at me," Frances said quietly. "I didn't do anything."

Josie shook her head. "I'm sorry," she said, feeling like she was about to start crying. She knelt next to the dirty splotches on the carpet and positioned the dustpan.

"I was just thinking," Frances said, starting over. "Maybe Sheriff Parnell will let me dust a fingerprint from the kitchen or somewhere. Do you think he would?"

Josie did not answer. She could only stare at the soiled rag in her hand. There was no manure on it. Only a fine black sand.

CHAPTER ELEVEN

"I hear a car in the yard," Frances said as Josie straightened up, the dustpan in her hand. Josie listened, hoping she was wrong.

"It's probably Sheriff Parnell," Frances said, and the excitement in her voice was unmistakable.

Josie hurried to the kitchen, eager to dump the black grit before Frances noticed it. When she turned to put the dustpan back on its hook in the broom closet, she heard her father opening the front door.

"Thanks for coming, Pete," he called out.

"It is him!" Frances said from the hall, leaning into the kitchen to whisper.

"I know," Josie told her, trying hard to figure out what to do. She needed to talk to her brother without anyone else around. "You go on out and watch," Josie said to Frances. "I'll go find Tom before he manages to lose himself in one of the barns again."

Frances nodded eagerly and headed toward the front door. Josie turned in the opposite direction, hurrying down the hall to cross the sitting room, going out the back door almost at a run. She cut straight across to the cow barn and opened the door to duck inside. The dim interior made her blink, her eyes still dazzled by the late afternoon sun.

"Tom?"

"Over here."

The quick answer startled Josie, and she turned to see her brother's shadowy form against the far wall. He was sitting on a bale of hay. She started toward him.

"Don't, Josie," he said quietly. "Please just leave me alone."

The sad tone of his voice made Josie feel sorry for him for a few seconds, then she found herself getting angry. "The sheriff is here and—"

"I know," Tom said. "I saw him drive up."

Josie stared at him. "You did?"

Tom nodded.

"You weren't out here when I was calling for you, were you? You lied to Daddy."

He was quiet for a long time, then he lifted his head. "Just leave me alone, Josie."

She couldn't see his face, but his voice was still strained. Josie glanced back at the barn door. She could see the slanting evening sun coming through the crack. "Were there hoboes? Did you feed them or something?"

Tom didn't answer.

Josie clenched her fists. She wanted an explanation. "Tom, I saw you doing *something*."

He looked up but didn't speak. Now that her eyes were adjusting to the dim light, Josie could see that his face was bleak, his mouth a thin line.

"I was awake and I looked out my window. I saw you carrying something. I thought you were probably feeding some hoboes dinner, but then—"

"You weren't awake," Tom snapped.

Josie ducked her head. "I was, too. I just didn't answer you."

Tom made a low, angry sound and stood up. "And you followed me out the creek path today and you—"

"I didn't *follow* you," Josie cut him off. "I just thought you might be up there."

"Why?" Tom's voice was a hoarse whisper. "Why would you think that?"

"Because I know you have some kind of secret place up there," Josie admitted in a low voice. "I thought maybe you would just need to get off by yourself, and I—"

Tom laughed, and it was such a cracked, strange sound that Josie fell silent. When he stopped, she could hear him breathing hard, like he had been running.

"You stole the gas, didn't you?" Josie said softly. "Did you want to take Evelyn somewhere?"

There was a long silence. Josie could hear her

brother breathing, but he had turned his face away, and she couldn't read his expression. "I gave Evelyn the gas," he said finally. "Her mother has been sick, and they wanted to take her to a doctor in Seattle."

"Tom, Daddy would have given them the gas if he had known that. What are you doing?" she demanded. "Did you break into the Buick? Why? If you wanted extra gas—"

"I didn't even know the gas was in there. I wanted the tent."

Josie felt her stomach clench. "The tent," she repeated woodenly. Nothing was making sense. "And the guns?" she whispered. "Why did you hide those bullets?"

He finally shuffled his feet and stood up. "They should have let me into the army."

Josie stared at him.

"They won't take me, Josie. I have flat feet."

His voice was so full of pain that Josie flinched. He didn't say anything for so long that she finally swallowed hard and pulled in a long breath. "Flat feet? I've heard people joke, but—"

"It's no joke," Tom said, cutting her off. "It means I can't march or something. My feet never hurt," he added bitterly. "I work all day, and my feet never hurt. I walk all over and—" He broke off, pulling in a long breath.

"Did you tell them that?" Josie asked him.

"I told them," Tom said. "I told them I could run faster than anyone in my class. I told them I was a good shot and I—"

"Tom," Josie began without any idea what she would say next.

But he only shook his head and held up one hand to silence her. "Josie, they took all my friends. I don't just mean Phil and Larry, I mean all of them, every single one. They took guys that will never be as good a soldier as I could have been."

Josie had no idea what to say, so she held very still, hoping that her father would not come looking for them now.

"They take men who are too old and too fat, but they won't take me," Tom whispered bitterly. "No, I have to stay here and see people looking at me sideways every day because they think—"

Tom made a choking sound. Then, abruptly, he shoved himself to his feet and pushed past her. He banged the door open and stumbled outside, leaving it standing open behind him. The sunlight streamed in, hazed with hay dust.

For a few seconds, Josie could only stare after him, then she ran to catch up. He was halfway to the hay shed, and his hunched shoulders told her that he was still close to crying as she ran up behind him and grabbed at his sleeve. He spun around to face her. "Leave me alone, Josie."

"No," Josie said, breathing hard. "Tom, you can just tell Daddy the truth. He'll understand how upset you are and—" She broke off when he wheeled around to face her.

"I took your key. I took the gas and the tent and the tools—and I stole his guns, Josie. His guns. And I have lied, and now my fingerprints . . . Dad is never going to forgive me for any of this. He already thinks I'm a coward and—" Tom broke off, his face distorted with an ugly grimace.

Josie stood still, stunned into silence. Then she inhaled sharply. "Sheriff Parnell will find your fingerprints."

Tom looked aside. "I wiped them all off. I think. I had to run when I saw him coming."

Tom closed his eyes. "This is all so crazy," he said. "I just wanted to go live—" he broke off and waved one hand vaguely toward the wooded hills off to the west, then cleared his throat again. "I just wanted to go where no one would look at me and think I was a coward."

"No one thinks that," Josie said quickly.

He glared at her. "You think it! You and your perfect garden and your scrap drives. Don't you think I know what you're so ashamed of?"

Josie could not meet his eyes. He glared at her as she glanced downward, then past him, trying to think of something to say. It was true: She had been ashamed of him. "I thought you were just waiting until you had to go," Josie began.

"I almost did," Tom said softly. "Josie, when they told me they wouldn't take me, for a second, I was *glad*." Tears rolled down his cheeks, and he wrenched around to face away from her.

"Tom, anybody would feel that, I think. I would. I—"

"You're a girl." Tom said it in a low, even voice, and she knew he was right. What she thought she would feel in his position didn't matter at all right now.

"I just never thought Dad would call the sheriff," Tom said. "I thought he'd just start making everyone lock the doors and—"

"Tom, you have to tell Daddy the truth now—"

"How am I going to break it to him that his only son is stupid?" Tom demanded. "I took the guns out this morning because I thought as long as the sheriff was coming, I'd better make it look real. And I thought—"

He stopped and swiped at his eyes. Josie waited, glancing toward the side yard. She didn't know how long it would take to dust for fingerprints, but it wouldn't be long before Daddy came looking for Tom, she was sure. He followed her glance and nodded. "I'd better get out of here." He sighed. "When I took the guns, I told myself that if the Japanese army invaded,

I'd be a hero up in the hills, fighting them off." He rubbed one hand over his tear-streaked face. "I've been thinking and acting like a ten-year-old kid."

Josie could only stare at him for a few seconds. Then she shook her head. "I know how bad it made you feel when Evelyn broke things off, and I know—"

"No, you don't, Josie. You can't imagine what it's like to be a man and not be able to fight in this war."

"Please tell Daddy the truth now," she whispered.

"Josie, just don't tell him anything," he pleaded. "I'll be gone by tomorrow morning."

"Josie? Are you back here?" Frances's voice shattered Josie's thoughts. "Josie? Tom?"

"Don't tell Dad anything," Tom repeated fiercely, "except that I will be there in a few minutes. Promise." Staring into her eyes, he gripped her arm so tightly that it hurt. "Promise me, Josie." She nodded.

Tom released her arm and sprinted toward the hay shed, rounding the corner at a dead run. Josie could only stand rooted to the ground, watching him go.

Frances was coming around the corner of the house. Josie could just see her through the lilacs, turning toward the machine shed, still calling their names.

"Over here," Josie shouted, walking toward her.

Frances looked annoyed. "Where's Tom?" Josie

struggled to find something to say. When she couldn't, she just started walking.

Frances had to run a few steps to catch up. "Sheriff Parnell's about to dust for fingerprints, but your father made me come look for you two."

Josie exhaled as she headed around the lilac bushes into the side yard. There had to be a way to end all this, to make it so Tom could tell Daddy what had happened, and why. She shivered, thinking about Tom sitting alone in his secret place with two guns and his bag of bullets. He was feeling so desperate, so awful. She didn't think he would hurt himself, but she wasn't sure of anything anymore. And if Daddy got angry enough at Tom, it would break his heart.

"Hurry up," Sheriff Parnell called out the minute he saw them coming. Then he touched his hat to greet Josie.

Daddy was standing a little ways off, his thumbs hooked in his belt, a thoughtful expression on his face. "Where's your brother?" he shouted.

Josie gestured back along the side yard. "He said to tell you he'd be here in a few minutes," she called back.

Frances ran the last fifty feet. Josie let her go, glancing at her father, trying to think.

"Come and watch, Josie," Frances said. "Hurry up."

Josie came to a stop beside the old Buick just as Sheriff Parnell opened a small wooden box. He lifted out a narrow-topped jar, then a small, puffy-looking paintbrush. Carefully, he dusted the Buick's door handle with a fine white powder.

"Nothing here," he said after a minute. "That means they were smart enough to wipe their prints off, or they never even tried the door."

Frances tilted her head. "They would, though," she said as he walked around to the far side of the car and began dabbing the dust on the opposite side. "Anyone would check to see if it was locked and if there were any valuables in the car before they broke the trunk lock, wouldn't they?"

Sheriff Parnell shrugged. "You'd think so. But criminals aren't always logical."

Tom's not a criminal, Josie wanted to shout. *He just wanted to run away.*

Sheriff Parnell was moving around to the back of the Buick now, taking his little box with him. He shook the powder out of the brush with precise little movements. Josie held her breath. "One print," he announced. "But it is a little blurred."

"There you are," Josie heard her father say. She looked up. Tom was coming around the house, his face set and tense.

"Only one print," Frances called out to him. "And it's blurred."

"No, wait," Sheriff Parnell said suddenly, "here's another. And it's as clear as daylight."

Josie saw Tom's face blanch, but he kept his expression blank as he walked toward them.

"Of course, unless they have a match on file up in Spokane, we won't really have anything to go on," Sheriff Parnell said.

Josie felt herself relaxing. Of course. Tom had no criminal record. There would be no matches on file anywhere.

"I'll just get a set from each of you before I leave," Sheriff Parnell was saying. "I'd hate to send them a print from one of you."

Daddy frowned. "That would be the crowning touch on all this whole infuriating mess—wasting everyone's time."

"That's why I want to make sure," Sheriff Parnell answered.

"But anyone who would steal a gun might have been smart enough to wipe his prints clean, though, Pete."

Sheriff Parnell nodded. "Prints outside like this can last a few months, even through some harsh weather."

"No one's been in that trunk since hunting season last year," Daddy said flatly. "So more like nine months."

"Nine months ago? That's long enough to mean anything we find will be a usable print," Sheriff Parnell said. "But I'll still take a set from the three of you if you don't mind," he added, and one from Mrs. Poe when she gets back."

Daddy nodded. "Makes no difference to me."

"Have you had any hired hands over the past few months?" Sheriff Parnell asked.

Daddy shook his head. "We only hire at harvest."

Josie looked at her brother. His eyes were narrowed, and he was even paler than he had been before.

CHAPTER TWELVE

"I'm glad you're here," Sheriff Parnell was saying to Tom.

Josie watched Tom blink, then nod.

"I just wanted to ask if you heard or saw anything unusual last night." Sheriff Parnell was taking out a square of dark paper. Without looking up at Tom, he pressed the paper on the print. When he pulled it away, Josie could see the whorls and spirals of the print on it. She glanced at her brother. His eyes were wide.

"He's going to take your fingerprints, too," Frances said excitedly.

"To make sure these are from the thief," Josie explained quickly.

"No one has had a reason to open the trunk since hunting season, your father tells me," Sheriff Parnell said.

Josie could see Tom trying to think, trying to figure out what to say. If he said now that he thought he might have opened the trunk, Daddy would want to know why he hadn't said so long before this.

"That right?" Sheriff Parnell asked.

"That's right," Tom said. "As far as I can remember, anyway. It's been most of a year."

"You haven't gone camping," Daddy said. "I haven't, either. I think we probably have a real thief's print there."

Sheriff Parnell straightened up. "That's certainly what I'm hoping." He turned. "Let me just get the ink pad out of my car, and we can do your prints while I talk to Tom."

"You want us back in the house, then?" Daddy asked.

Sheriff Parnell nodded. "The kitchen would be fine. Then you can wash the ink off quick. It stains." He started for his car, then looked back. "Frances, you don't touch anything, please."

Frances glanced at Josie, blushing. "I won't."

"Let's go on in, then," Daddy said, and Josie began to walk, her heart thudding in her chest.

Tom hesitated. "I just remembered I left the pasture gate open," he said suddenly. "I'll be back in a minute."

"Hurry up with it," Daddy said irritably. "Sheriff Parnell won't be able to stay much longer. He has his own supper to get to."

Sheriff Parnell laughed. "And I am sure you do, too."

Josie felt her stomach tighten. She hadn't even thought about supper. Mama would have. She always made sure there was good, hot food, no matter what else went wrong. Josie felt her eyes stinging as she turned to follow her father and Sheriff Parnell.

If Mama had been here, none of this would have happened. She would have heard Tom sneaking around, and she would have gotten up and talked to him. Then she would have talked to Daddy and told him about Tom being rejected by the army.

Josie looked back to see her brother swallow hard, staring at Sheriff Parnell's back as he walked toward his car. Tom saw Josie watching and he lifted his right hand, waving, before he turned to start toward the back of the house again.

"Oh, this is so exciting," Frances said, coming close to hook her arm through Josie's. "I mean, I am really sorry that it all happened, but you have to admit—"

"Hurry along, you two," Daddy called from the front walk.

"We can talk about it later," Josie said.

Frances nodded and broke into a run, pulling Josie along with her. When they got to the steps, Josie slowed and pulled herself free, following Frances into the kitchen. A few seconds later, Sheriff Parnell came in, another little box in his hand. He laid out an ink pad and a stack of thick white paper. There were little boxes inked on the paper, and lines for the person's name and address.

Daddy went first. Josie kept glancing at the doorway, watching for Tom, wishing he would just come in and tell everyone the truth. It would be bad, but not as bad as what was going to happen if he tried to keep lying about everything.

"Josie, you're next," Daddy said, standing up from the chair. "Then you can start supper." He held out his ink-stained hand, looking at it. "Where in blazes is your brother?"

"Maybe he had to chase cows in," Josie said quickly.

"If I can't question him tonight, I want him to come down to the office in the morning, first thing," Sheriff Parnell said.

Daddy grunted an assent as Josie sat in the chair. She saw him glancing toward the front door. She could tell he was thinking about going to find Tom himself.

"Daddy?" Josie said brightly. "Frances and I were thinking about trying to run a scrap drive."

"They were telling me a little about it in the car on the way out here this afternoon," Sheriff Parnell said amiably.

"Scrap drive?" Daddy said. He didn't sound like he was really listening.

"We wanted to do something important," Josie said, thinking about Tom's face, how miserable he had looked. Sheriff Parnell picked up her hand and rolled her index finger over the ink pad. Then he pressed it onto the first square on the white paper, rolling it from left to right, then lifted it straight up. He took her middle finger and started over.

Frances insisted on being fingerprinted, and Josie kept talking about the scrap drive as she bustled around, putting together a meat loaf with enough oats mixed in to make the meat go further. By the time it was in the oven, Sheriff Parnell was putting away his fingerprint equipment, and Daddy was frowning.

"I don't know where he took off to, Sheriff," he apologized. "I'll bring him in the morning, you have my word."

"Someone said he's having girlfriend trouble," Sheriff Parnell said. "I can remember what that was like."

"It's no excuse," Daddy said. "I don't know what's gotten into him."

Josie peeled potatoes while her father walked Sheriff Parnell out to the car. Frances helped, and Josie tried to talk a little about the scrap drive, but it was hard. She could not stop remembering Tom's little wave. She was pretty sure she knew what it meant, so she made a decision. She thought it was the one Mama would have made, but it still wasn't easy. The minute her father came back in, she turned to face him. "Daddy?"

"What, Josie? When will supper be ready?" He sounded impatient, and she hesitated, taking a deep breath.

"Frances is going to finish making the gravy. I want to show you something."

"Show me something?" he exploded. "Josie, I don't have time right now to—"

"Just for a minute, Daddy, please," she interrupted him.

She waited and held her breath until he nodded.

"All right, all right. But make it quick. I want to go find your brother. There's no excuse for him being rude to the sheriff like this."

Josie nodded, leading him outside. She was thinking furiously. The only way to solve anything was to have Tom talk honestly with Daddy—and she was pretty sure that wasn't going to happen unless she *made* it happen, tonight. Tom was going to leave, she had no doubt. That's what his sad little wave had meant. He had been saying good-bye to her.

"I think I have this all figured out," Josie said as they walked into the backyard.

"What?" He sounded impatient.

"It was off this way, I think," Josie said, stopping at the fence. As if she was just trying to see better, she climbed through the wire and walked a dozen paces out into the pasture.

"What did you see?" Daddy demanded.

Josie glanced back but didn't answer him. She made her eyes go wide and pretended to be staring at something.

"What is it?"

She still didn't answer, and out of the corner of her eye she saw her father bending to duck through the fence wire. He hurried toward her, and she turned to answer him. "I'm not sure. I think it was Tom."

Daddy shook his head. "You think?"

"Maybe. He might have had the same thought I just did, Daddy. He might be going up the creek, too." She turned to face her father and let out a huge breath. "He's probably got all this figured out, too." She put one hand over her mouth, feigning surprise. "I'll bet we're right!" She started walking as fast as she could, then began to run. She could hear her father running behind her.

"Josie?" he called after they had crossed the pasture and started up the creek bed. "Where are you taking me? What's this about?"

He sounded so angry that Josie slowed a little, but she stayed far enough ahead that he had to keep walking. "You remember that old secret place of Tom's?" She glanced back. "I bet that's where the hoboes are."

Daddy shook his head. "Secret place?"

"His old fort, where he used to sneak off when he was younger," Josie said over her shoulder.

"I never knew anything about it," Daddy said. She could hear him breathing hard now, but she kept up the pace. The tone of his voice was changing. He sounded puzzled. "Josie, what in the devil is going on?"

"I think Tom had the same idea I just had," Josie explained without slowing down even a little.

Daddy didn't answer for a few seconds. The path was getting steeper, and the black, gritty sand was deep underfoot. "What idea?" he finally asked.

Josie waited until they were coming around the last curve of the creek bed, in sight of the cottonwood trees, before she answered. "I bet he decided that his old secret place would be the perfect spot for hoboes to live." She began to run again, getting a ways in front of her father before he realized what she was doing and started calling her name.

"Josie? If there are men up here—" he shouted. Then he called her name again. "Josie!"

"Tom?" Josie shouted frantically at the rocky hillside as she ran beneath the old spreading trees. It was almost dusk, and the shadows beneath them were ink dark. "Tom, I told Daddy that the hoboes might be up here!"

There was no answer as Daddy came to a stop beside her.

"Tom!!" she shouted at the top of her lungs. "Did you find anything? Did the hoboes put the tent up there?"

Daddy stood close beside her, breathing hard from the uphill run, his face contorted with a worried frown. "Josie, if there are men camping up here—"

"Tom!" she screamed at the hillside. "Tom, answer me! Did you find any of the stolen goods up there?"

When she stopped yelling, a silence settled over the little valley. Josie crossed her fingers behind her back, counting seconds as they went past. She was up to seven when Tom's voice came from the hillside before them. "Josie? Is that you?"

"Yes," she shouted back, her heart beating fast. "Did you find any of the stolen stuff? Did the hoboes camp out here?"

"Where is he?" Daddy asked, and she turned to see him squinting as Tom answered.

"Yes," Tom shouted back, and his voice was tight and strained. "Yes, Josie, they did."

Josie let out a whoosh of breath. Her eyes stung, and she was afraid she might start crying.

"How do we get up there?" Daddy yelled.

"There's a path," Tom called, and for the first time he stepped forward so that they could see him. He pointed off to their left. Daddy started off, and Josie followed him.

The secret place was almost exactly as Josie had pictured it. It was a natural cave that Tom had widened. He had rearranged things while they were climbing up the steep path, she was sure. In the shadowy light that came in through the entrance, she saw what had probably been a neat bedroll. It was now a pile of soiled cloth. The guns were lying willy-nilly on the floor, and the cracked bowl rested on the dirt floor next to a broken table.

"They probably saw the sheriff's car today and took off for the hills," Daddy said, looking around, beaming. "Tom, I'm glad you got to the bottom of this!"

"It was Josie's idea, too," Tom reminded him, and Josie smiled at her brother as Daddy slapped him on the back.

"How do hoboes avoid the draft, Daddy?" Josie asked suddenly.

Her father shook his head. "I don't know. I suppose they just keep moving. It would be a lonely life." He glanced at Tom. "I've been thinking about the draft for weeks because of you. You know, Jerry Frink says if you enlist, you get more choices about where you'll end up."

Tom glanced at Josie, and she closed her eyes, hoping he would just tell the truth.

"I tried to enlist three weeks ago, Dad," he said in a small voice.

Daddy turned around. "You what?"

"I tried to enlist," Tom repeated in the same low voice.

"Tried," Daddy repeated.

"They wouldn't take me, Dad. I have flat feet, they said."

Josie watched a quick parade of expressions pass over her father's face. He looked astonished, then angry, then wistful and finally relieved. "I don't know what to say, Tom," he began, his voice trembling. "I am sorry, but I'm glad, too. I kept thinking about you dying over there in some muddy field—"

Tom didn't speak. He just stood silently with his arms straight down at his sides. But Josie could see tears glittering in his eyes.

"You're a farmer. That's a big contribution to the war, son. Food is ammunition in times like these."

Tom's face still looked bleak and pale, Josie noticed, but he was smiling uncertainly. "I think I'd better go make sure Frances doesn't burn the gravy," she said.

Tom and Daddy were looking at each other, their eyes intense and careful. Josie backed up, then bent to pass beneath the low arch of stone that made an entrance to the cave. All the way back to the house, she skipped, then ran, then hopped, then ran again, humming to herself the whole way.

She had done it! Daddy and Tom were talking,

and it had looked like they would keep talking. Josie was sure her mother would be proud of her, even though she had fibbed to get them to start talking. As she bent to take off her shoes and dump the black grit into the flower bed next to the door, Josie smelled dinner and her mouth watered.

"The gravy came out fine," Frances said as she came into the kitchen.

Josie smiled. "Thank you for helping, Frances," she said. Then, still humming happily to herself, she started setting the table.

July 15, Friday night and Tom is out with Evelyn. He told her about his 4F rating, and she said she was relieved, too, that she had been afraid to fall in love with someone who might not live through the war. Tom can't believe it. Evelyn is probably the only girl in Palouse who sees the war as a small part of their future together. She does think Tom should move to Spokane and work in a munitions factory or something. That's what she wants to do now, she says. Maybe even Seattle.

Mama called tonight, and Daddy told her about Tom's 4F. She cried on the phone. She had no trouble saying she was glad he wouldn't have to go!!

Mama said she will be home a day early, and I can't wait for Monday to come!! I am so tired of cooking and cleaning up, I could throw up!!! I think I will try to find a man who doesn't mind helping out with some of the housework. Mama says there are some men like that, though not many.

Tom has offered to help us with whatever we decide to do for a scrap drive. That will make a big difference. He will be able to pick up big loads with the truck. Frances and I are talking about how to work things out so that we can get more scrap than anyone ever has!

God, before I go to sleep, thank you for helping me get Tom out of trouble over everything that *happened. You won't be sorry. And I would like to pray again, like I do every night, that this lousy war will be over before too much longer. No one wants it to go on, do they?*

Sometimes one day can change a life forever

American Diaries

**Different girls,
living in different periods of America's past
reveal their hearts' secrets in the pages
of their diaries. Each one faces a challenge
that will change her life forever.
Don't miss any of their stories:**

www.SimonSaysKids.com